CULPEPPER'S REBELLION

LORI CRANE

Published by Lori Crane Entertainment
Cover design: Robert Hess
Editor: Elyse Dinh-McCrillis

www.LoriCrane.com

This book is a work of historical fiction.
Some names, characters, places, and incidents are from historical
accounts.
Some names, characters, places, and incidents are products of the
author's imagination.

ISBN: 978-0996429511
eBook ISBN: 978-0996429528

FAMILY LINEAGE/CAST

OF CHARACTERS

John Culpepper 1606-

John's wife: Mary Culpepper
John's son: John "Johnny" Culpepper 1644-
John's niece: Frances Culpepper Stephens
Berkeley 1634-
Frances's husband: Sir William Berkeley 1605-
1677
John's nephew: Alex Culpepper 1632-

Residents of Virginia and Carolina:

Nathaniel Bacon 1647-1676
William Drummond 1617-1677
George Durant 1632-
Valentine Bird ?-1679
Thomas Miller 1649-1685

Culpepper's Rebellion

Table of Contents

1. 1680, The Tower, London   7
2. Ten Years Earlier, 1670,
      Green Spring Plantation   11
3. 1673, Taxation   25
4. Albemarle, Carolina   33
5. August 1674, Nathaniel Bacon   39
6. July 1675, Doeg Indians   45
7. Maryland Indians   55
8. January 1676,
      Susquehanna Indians   61
9. Drummond Resigns   65
10. Indians and News Wives   71
11. Berkeley's Retreat   83
12. Bacon's Sloop   87
13. Berkeley's Opening Address   97
14. Bacon's Invasion   105
15. Accomac, Virginia   113
16. King Charles II   117
17. Revolt Over   125
18. Spring 1677,
       Return to Green Spring   127
19. Albemarle, Carolina   135
20. Berkeley Summoned   139
21. Kidnap   143
22. Green Spring   147

23. Election	151
24. Albemarle	155
25. 1678, Miller Escapes	159
26. December 1679, Treason	165
27. Intervention	169
28. Lord Shaftesbury	173
29. Trial of Johnny Culpepper	177
30. Home	187
Author's Notes	191
Books by Lori Crane	197
About the Author	199
Excerpt from *Okatibbee Creek*	201

CHAPTER 1

1680, The Tower, London

John followed the guard down the winding hallway. It was narrow and dark with only the light of an occasional torch resting in its iron holder, flickering shadows on the stone walls. Where John could see, the walls looked dark and damp, covered with a slimy layer of green mold, but the musty smell didn't mask the overwhelming stench of urine and feces. He shook his head and wrinkled his nose at the insult.

As he passed intermittent arched doorways, prisoners yelled at him through small, bar-covered windows and pounded their fists on the wooden doors. Some begged for mercy, others pleaded for food and drink. The desperate voices echoing off the walls should have made John uneasy, but he only felt sheer hopelessness for those imprisoned. He didn't look up when they called to him. He walked behind the guard with his head down, his heart heavy. How could any man endure this dreadful place? He remembered his older brother serving a short sentence within these walls during the civil war more than thirty years earlier, but in all of John's seventy-four years, he had never seen the inside of the Tower. The unfortunate occasion that had brought him all the way from Virginia to be here on this day was more terrifying than the actual place.

The guard slowed when he rounded the corner, reaching inside his tunic pocket and noisily producing a ring of iron keys. John waited while the man found the appropriate key and placed it in the keyhole. When he turned it, there was a loud metallic snap. The guard pushed open the door, which moaned softly on its rusted hinges, and John entered.

The small room was lit by only a sliver of a window placed so high on the wall that none could see in or out. As the guard closed and locked the door behind him, John's heart melted at the sight of the figure lying in a ball on a wooden platform, facing the moldy wall. John assumed the platform was a bed, but there was no blanket, no warmth, no comfort. A mouse scampered across John's boot and disappeared into the tiniest of holes in the wall. At least the prisoners didn't have to sleep on the floor with the mice.

"Johnny?" John said quietly.

Johnny sat up and spun around. "Father! What are you doing here?"

"I came to see to your welfare."

"They've charged me with treason." He ran his fingers through his disheveled curls.

"I know. That's why I'm here." His son looked so thin and worn. "You need a lawyer and I know of none better than myself."

"You hate practicing law."

"I'd hate it more to see your head on the scaffold."

"I don't think you can prevent it. They believe I embezzled the king's funds."

"Did you?"

"Of course not."

"Then we'll find a way out of this. Your mother will be very displeased with me if I allow you to lose your head."

Johnny rose and wrapped his arms around John. "Thank you for coming, Father. I hate to admit it..." He paused and swallowed hard. "But for the first time in my life, I'm truly frightened."

"I am too, son."

CHAPTER 2

Ten Years Earlier, 1670, Green Spring Plantation

After John's thirty-four-year-old niece Frances married his sixty-five-year-old friend Governor William Berkeley, the newlyweds set up house in Berkeley's massive estate, Green Spring. The one-thousand-acre sprawling plantation was fronted by a long drive, referred to as Sugar Row, which was shaded by lofty pecan trees and sugar maples. The front lawn of the stately house hosted clumps of fragrant mulberry and honey locust. Behind the house grew acres and acres of corn, wheat, barley, rye, and tobacco, standing tall like sentinels as far as the eye could see. Since the property was located only three miles from Jamestown, Berkeley ventured into town daily to see to his gubernatorial responsibilities, leaving his new wife in charge of running the plantation, which she did exquisitely. She commanded twenty-three servants and slaves, and John had a suspicion that Green Spring plantation would make more money this year than it had in years past. Frances knew how to get things done. Following their marriage, Berkeley's standing in the community seemed to be expanding as well, for Frances was the grand dame of hosting galas and luncheons. She charmed even the most inflexible of Berkeley's rivals.

John and Berkeley had attended Middle Temple in their youths. Neither had emerged from the prestigious law school with a seat on the bench, as Berkeley had moved to the colonies and John had bought a ship. Berkeley served at the governor of Virginia and John ran a merchant business between London and Virginia, seeing his friend only on rare occasions. Following a disastrous civil war in England, and John, being a devout royalist, found his merchant business abruptly halted when Parliament transformed England into the English Commonwealth. Not being able to run his ship out of London any longer, he moved his family to Virginia and found himself practicing law to support his family. For the last twenty years, John had advised Berkeley in the legalities of colonial business, but he found the daily business of governing the colony a time-consuming and tedious endeavor, and Berkeley seldom listened to him anyway.

Berkeley had become quite crusty and stodgy in his old age, and had developed an annoying habit of tapping on his chin with his fingertips. John didn't know why the man did that. So many times he wanted to yell, "Stop that!" but he knew raising his voice to Berkeley would only made his friend more nervous, which increased the tapping tenfold. Strangely, in their youth, John never thought Berkeley a nervous or frightened person, but the older Berkeley got, the more John saw signs that Berkeley lived in a constant state of fear. Fear of failure, fear of the unknown, and mostly, fear of indecision.

Lately, John had been frustrated that he couldn't get the man to see reason. Their legal conversations would begin with Berkeley questioning everything while he tapped his chin, and often ended with Berkeley waving his hand at John and doing what he wanted without taking John's opinion to heart. That was one of the things John hated about practicing law. It was seldom black and white. The truth was always in the eye of the beholder, and Berkeley's vision changed and ebbed as public opinion altered. The anxiety over public scrutiny was one of Berkeley's greatest fears.

Though John had always despised practicing law, upon the death of Frances's first husband, Governor Samuel Stephens, she became the sole heir to all of Stephens's lands and plantations, including the thirteen-hundred-acre Boldrup Plantation in Virginia and the island of Roanoke. John had no choice but to step forward to protect Frances's interests, and he did so willingly, occasionally even feeling a rare and slight gratitude that his father had made him attend law school in his youth.

To the dismay of John's father, Johannes, John didn't follow the plans his father had laid out. He didn't become a practicing lawyer, serve in Parliament, or become the respected country gentleman Johannes expected. John spent his early adulthood as a merchant, sailing back and forth between Virginia and London, a way of life his father condemned. They never settled their differences. Johannes died during John's first voyage. Years later, as John smuggled his family out of England following the war, he wondered if his father would have finally been proud of him. He doubted it.

In 1650, John, his brother Thomas, and their families settled on the eastern peninsula of Virginia, a small town called Accomac. It was a quaint fishing village with only a population of a few hundred on the east side of the Chesapeake Bay, a day's ride and sail to Jamestown. Just as the family was beginning to feel comfortable in their new land, Thomas died in Virginia in 1652. John reluctantly stepped into his older brother's role of family patriarch, watching over his nieces and nephews. With England's political landscape still in chaos and John's sailing days behind him, he settled into a mundane life in Virginia, using his legal skills to protect his family and to assist Berkeley.

The youngest of his brother's children, Frances, had become the most affluent dame in the colonies, rising to prominence during her seventeen-year marriage to Governor Stephens. Her ascension wasn't halted by her husband's untimely death. She was adored by the people, and they continued to cherish her with or without the title of first lady.

A year after Stephens's death, she married Governor William Berkeley and continued her social prominence. Her new title was Lady Frances Berkeley, first lady of Virginia. She rose to the occasion, constantly hosting an array of visitors at Green Spring who wished her favor. She was an attractive woman with a willowy figure and smoky eyes, and her marital status didn't deter unscrupulous admirers. It was obvious she enjoyed the attention, generally emitting an air of grandeur and importance that other ladies in Virginia might consider haughty, but Frances didn't worry herself with her image among the womenfolk of Jamestown, only with her standing among the prominent businessmen and politicians.

It seemed to John that many of these

guests visited Green Spring more frequently than they visited Berkeley's office at the state house. Since Berkeley spent most of his time in Jamestown on colony business and Frances's political connections and personal wealth made her ripe for the attention of unprincipled gentlemen, John had taken it upon himself to act the protector of his niece and her money.

John had recently returned from London on family business and after not seeing each other for months, Frances invited John to Green Spring for a luncheon. She also demanded her husband stay home so they could enjoy a quiet afternoon and catch up on the latest news from England. Neither John nor Berkeley ever wanted to disappoint Frances, so they obliged her request. John knew the conversation with Berkeley would eventually turn to colonial business, but he was hoping to have a little time to visit with his beloved niece.

As predicted, it didn't take long for the conversation to sway to the latest happenings in the House of Burgesses, specifically Berkeley's plan to change the poll tax to include not only land owners but all men of the colony, whether they be sons, servants, sharecroppers, or slaves.

"Will, you can't push that act through the House. The people of Virginia can't afford any more taxation. They're already taxed enough," John said as they took their seats in the opulent dining room.

"What difference does it make?" Berkeley ran his sausage-shaped fingers through his frizzy hair. "The poor still get the benefit of the vote, so they should have to pay the poll tax also. Why should only land owners be burdened with the expense?"

A servant girl wearing a crisp, white apron eased around them and poured brandy into their crystal goblets.

"Poor people already spend nearly half their income paying your current taxes. That's why it's impossible for them to become land owners."

Berkeley stared straight ahead as if considering John's statement. He tapped on his chin with his fingers. After a moment, he waved his hand at John's statement as if to brush it off. "Poor people still make an income off the land, even if they're only sharecroppers. They have plenty of land to raise crops and therefore to pay the poll tax. Besides, what else are they going to do? Revolt? Maybe if they don't have enough money to own land or pay taxes, they shouldn't live here. They should go back to England and pay taxes there. See? They'll pay wherever they go. They really don't have a choice."

Frances waltzed into the dining room, followed by two servant girls carrying overloaded trays of meats and cheeses. "Lunch is served, gentlemen," she announced, her smile brightening the room.

"Good. I'm starving," Berkeley gruffed as he tucked his napkin into the neck of his shirt.

Frances stood next to her chair waiting for someone to pull it out for her. John watched Berkeley for a moment, but when he realized Berkeley was not going to assist her, John rose, walked around the table, and pulled out Frances's chair.

She smiled as she took her seat. "Thank you, Uncle."

John nodded, then returned to his chair and placed his napkin on his lap. "I don't know, Will. I think you're going to push and push until the colonists start pushing back."

"Are you men talking about business again? Let's have a nice, quiet lunch for a change," Frances said as she raised her arms and waited for the servant to place a napkin on her lap. Once the girl did so, Frances smoothed it out, ignoring the servant.

"You're absolutely correct, my dear," Berkeley smiled at her. "We'll curb our conversation for another time."

John exhaled in frustration, knowing the House of Burgesses had passed far too many taxes as of late and word in the colony was not favorable. The landowners struggled to pay taxes on themselves. How were they supposed to pay a poll tax on their sons, servants, and slaves? Many would lose their lands. The rich would get richer and the poor would get poorer.

Though the room became filled with the clinking sounds of forks against plates, John noticed his nephew was not eating. Frances's brother had not said a word to anyone since he and John arrived at Green Spring. Thirty-eight-year-old Alex had recently moved back to the colony after a lengthy stay in England and had been depressed and miserable since his return. John thought having lunch with Frances would cheer Alex up, but he was obviously mistaken. Alex fidgeted with his fork, picking at the food on the ornate china plate. He moved the braised carrots around in a circle but didn't take one bite. His brandy glass was empty, however, and the servant filled it for the third time.

"Alex," said Frances, "how did you end up becoming the surveyor general of Virginia? When did you decide to return to Virginia, and why didn't you let me know you were coming?"

John froze with his fork halfway to his mouth. He looked at Alex.

"Um...that's quite a long story, Sister. Perhaps another day we can discuss it," Alex replied. He glanced nervously at John.

"Oh, nonsense. Tell us now," she prodded. "I want to hear about everything that's been happening in England for the last eighteen years. You never wrote to me even once. I have no idea what you've been doing over there except Uncle John said you were living at Leeds Castle, tending to our cousin's wife."

John huffed. "Tending is a good word," he said under his breath.

Alex shot a glance toward him. "Uncle, this isn't the time or place."

"You can't hide the secret forever, Alex," John said.

Frances looked from her brother to her uncle and back with her eyebrows raised. She placed her fork down, sat up straight, and dabbed the corners of her mouth with her napkin. "Oh, now you have my interest piqued. What happened in England?"

Alex let out an exaggerated sigh and looked down at his plate. After a moment, he said, "Our cousin, Lord Thomas, appointed me surveyor general and sent me here to get me away from Margaretta, his wife."

Frances's eyes widened. "Did you have something adulterous happening with Lady Culpepper?"

"It wasn't adulterous," snapped Alex.

"Wait! Wait!" Frances threw her hands in the air in front of her. "Didn't she just have a child?"

Everyone froze like statues as they stared at Alex. Berkeley eyed his brother-in-law curiously. John held his breath. Even the servants stood stone-still against the tapestry-covered walls, pretending not to listen.

"Didn't she?" repeated Frances. "Yes, I'm certain I heard she gave birth to a daughter."

Alex and John glanced at each other, not knowing how much should be revealed to the chatty Frances. Not only would the entire colony learn the truth of the child's paternity by nightfall, but word would certainly spread to England within a short amount of time. No mere ocean could stop the gossip of the effervescent Lady Berkeley, especially if there might be something in it for her.

John finally spoke. "Yes, Margaretta delivered a daughter and Alex has moved back to Virginia. That's all anyone needs to know."

"She's yours, Alex?" Frances asked.

Alex's face was pale. He looked from his sister to his plate and nodded.

"I have a niece? How delightful! What's her name?" Frances was smiling ear to ear.

"Catherine," Alex said softly.

"Named after our mother?" Frances covered her chest with her hands and her expression softened. She looked as if tears would burst forth at any moment. "Oh, Alex, I'm thrilled," she said.

Alex shook his head. "No one needs to know, and you'll probably never meet her. She is Lady Catherine Culpepper, the daughter of Lord Thomas Culpepper, second baron of Thoresway, and that's the way it shall remain."

Frances pouted. "But I should love to see her." After a moment, she added, "And Lady Culpepper, too. Who is this woman who has stolen my brother's heart, enough for him to risk a family scandal?" Frances giggled.

Alex looked for a moment as if he might say something, but then he abruptly rose, nearly knocking his chair over, and stomped out of the room.

Frances shrugged at her uncle. "Why is he so upset?"

"I think he'd rather be in England with Margaretta and I'm certain he misses the baby," John said.

A servant picked up the chair and slid it to its appropriate place as Frances picked up her crystal goblet and took a sip. "Well, if Lord Thomas sent him here to keep him away from Margaretta, Alex needs to come to terms with that. There's not much he can do to compete with a baron. He doesn't have the social status. He could have at one point, but he never applied himself. I'm sure he'll find happiness here in Virginia — eventually."

Contrary to Frances's prediction, when John returned home to Accomac the next day, he found a letter penned by Alex:

Dearest Uncle,

I appreciate everything you've done for me, but I can no more live in denial of my daughter and my love for her mother than I can live without air to breathe. I have appointed an assistant to my position as surveyor general, and I am returning to England on the next available ship. I will certainly stay out of the way of Lord Thomas, but mark my words — I will die within the walls of Leeds Castle, within the arms of Lady Margaretta, with my daughter by my side. Please forgive me if you think I bring shame to the family. I don't believe true love is ever shameful.

> *With my deepest gratitude,*
> *Alex*

John frowned as he stared at the paper. His wife Mary reached out and touched his forearm. "John, I had a long talk with Alex this morning about returning to England. He truly loves Margaretta and the baby. I think it's the right thing for him to do."

John sighed. "I agree a man should be with the woman he loves, but it isn't possible if that woman is married to another. I can't deny him the love he feels, but I worry for him. Lord Thomas is not a rival to be challenged."

Mary patted his arm. "Alex is a grown man. He will make his own decisions."

Her dark eyes and sincere expression warmed John's heart. After thirty-eight years of marriage, five children, and living on two continents, there wasn't another woman in the world who held his heart the way Mary did. If Alex cared for Margaretta half as much as John cared for Mary, he couldn't blame Alex for going back to England to be with her. The odds of living a happy family life were against him with Margaretta's husband living nearby, but John couldn't deny it—he would do the same for Mary. Sadly, Alex could very well lose his head over this affair.

Without a word, John leaned over and kissed his wife.

CHAPTER 3

1673, Taxation

On a sunny fall morning, eight England-bound cargo ships converged on the James River, assembling before setting sail across the ocean. They were loaded with colonial tobacco, which would bring the planters of Virginia a healthy and substantial profit upon the ships' return later in the year. In the warm breeze, the ships raised their white sails and navigated the river, emerging into the sparkling, deep blue waters of Chesapeake Bay. Within moments of reaching the open waters, Dutch raiders attacked them. Cannon fire rang out as the raiders encircled the cargo vessels. Sailors pulled the sails tighter in an attempt to outrun the raiders, but they weren't prepared for a battle. Holes were blasted in the sides of the cargo ships. Gunfire shot across their bows and ripped their sails as the raiders moved closer and closer. Soon, the tobacco ships, hoisting only broken masts and limp sails hanging from damaged yardarms, slowed to a standstill, bobbing in the water like ducks. The battle was short lived. English sailors dove into the bay and swam toward shore. The raiders didn't pursue them. They seemed only interested in the ship's cargo. They seized all eight ships, stole the produce, then destroyed what was left of the vessels, sinking them into the bay.

John and Berkeley were sitting in Berkeley's office when a dripping wet sailor, panting and frantic, ran in and told them what had happened.

"Will, we need to do something about these raiders. I never ran across that kind of aggression when I sailed a merchant ship. The problem is getting worse and worse."

"I know it is, but I'm having trouble forming a militia to fight them off."

"What kind of trouble? We have thousands of men in the colony. Aren't they willing to fight?"

Berkeley shook his head, placed his elbow on the desk, and began tapping his chin. "We have six thousand, but honestly, they've been so angry lately over the taxes, I don't want to consider what would happen if we armed them. They'd probably turn the weapons I supply them back on me. I've actually been forced to hire armed guards just to assure my safe travels between the state house and Green Spring. And there are also six thousand servants and two thousand slaves in the colony, but no one has the desire to arm them, either."

"I wish you'd focus on one problem at a time. We need a solution to these Dutch raiders."

Berkeley looked at John. Tap, tap, tap.

John shook his head in exasperation.

The Dutch were an ongoing problem, the local Indians were a bigger problem, but in the last year, revolts from the colonists themselves were Berkeley's main concern. Melees had erupted three times over the last few months over taxation. Angry colonists had interrupted meetings of the general assembly, and some members of the House of Burgesses had been accosted on the roads while traveling to and from meetings.

The first revolt came when, against John's advice, Berkeley pushed the poll tax through. It was levied on each man in the colony over sixteen years of age, whether he be a land owner, a son, servant, or slave. Sixty pounds of tobacco per man was the cost. It was an exorbitant expense, but the cost wasn't the primary problem. The residents had been repeatedly driven from their land by the local Indians, only to return to destroyed crops. This sorely impeded their ability to pay the new poll tax, if not making it downright impossible.

The second revolt came after the previous Dutch raid, when as a consequence, the House of Burgesses passed the new Fort Tax. As Berkeley had just told John, he had also reported to the House that there was no way to raise a militia with the colonists as unsettled as they were, so the House figured the only way to keep the colony safe from the Dutch and the Indians was to build forts. With the elevated view from the well-manned forts, soldiers would be able to warn colonists of invasions and perhaps protect them. Steep taxes were raised and the building of the forts was planned, but the promised forts ended up being nothing more than mud and dirt huts that were never adequately manned and never of any use to anyone. The colonists felt they had been cheated by the contractors and by their own government—namely their aged governor.

The third revolt happened when, again against John's advice, Berkeley persuaded the Virginia General Assembly to exempt members of the court, legislature, and church vestries from the newly passed poll tax. Of course, Berkeley and his cohorts benefitted from the act, and the common people were livid.

Following the exemption, the assembly found itself needing to make up that deficit in taxes, so they passed the Plantation Duty Act. This tightened the belts of the colonists even further. It created an English monopoly on the

Virginia tobacco trade by taxing tobacco being shipped to neighboring colonies. This resulted in Virginia's neighbors trading with the Indians at a lower cost than with the planters of Virginia.

Again and again over the last three years, John had pleaded with Berkeley to use some common sense. He frequently heard rumblings in the community that the colonists couldn't take much more. Some even came directly to John, asking him to speak to the governor about the taxes. The economy was failing. Planters were losing their lands. Families were starving. John knew after watching the civil war come about in England that this was precisely how wars started. The people of Virginia had been pushed to their breaking point and would soon begin to push back. One could see it coming, like dark, storm clouds forming on the horizon. Berkeley, in his typical flair, dismissed all of John's concerns.

The final straw came when King Charles, in his promise to reward the Culpepper family for standing by him through his exile during the war, granted a thirty-one-year lease on the northern part of Virginia to John's cousin Lord Thomas. Five million acres of Virginia land was now owned by a baron who resided in England and had never once visited the colony. Even members of the Virginia assembly were upset about this intrusion. They petitioned the king to revoke the patent, and they even attempted to buy it from Lord Thomas. They pleaded with John to write to his cousin in England and come to some kind of agreement. John reluctantly did so on numerous occasions, but his letters were never returned. He even wrote to Lord Thomas's wife, Margaretta, but her response was she had not seen her husband in years and sadly could not be of any assistance.

The final outcome of the grant was that a large portion of Virginia now could not be settled without Lord Thomas's express permission. And if a colonist couldn't pay taxes on the land he already farmed, he would immediately forfeit the land to its owner—Lord Thomas. Seeing that the Indians' seemingly favorite pastime was destroying settlers' crops, the residents frequently found themselves unable to pay their taxes and losing their land to the absentee Lord Thomas.

If all of that wasn't bad enough, the tobacco tax raised by the Plantation Duty Act had worked so well at raising revenue, Berkeley and the assembly passed a new tax on *all* trade with other colonies—on leather, wool, fur, and hide. The local Indians didn't suffer the tax and sold furs and hides to the colonists in Maryland and New York for less money. As a result, northern merchants began refusing to trade anything with the colonists of Virginia, many of whom were doomed to homelessness.

The upset residents of Virginia would

soon be forced to take matters into their own hands. They couldn't do anything about taxes or trade, but they could do something about the Indians. Behind closed doors and without the knowledge of Berkeley or his assembly, they began arming themselves. They only needed to find someone to organize and lead them.

CHAPTER 4

Albemarle, Carolina

John took a few days off from the aggravation of counseling Berkeley to travel down to Albemarle, Carolina and check on his youngest son. Johnny, his namesake, had always been a precocious child, and he'd retained the same trait as a twenty-nine-year-old man. Johnny seldom returned home to Virginia, not even to visit his mother, so if John wanted to see him, he had to travel south. He had invited Mary to join him on the journey, but she said she wasn't feeling well and opted to stay home. She packaged some baked goods for her son and sent them with John, but John ate them before he even reached Carolina.

Johnny never stayed in one place long, and John new his son would never settle down or build a house. He didn't know exactly where to find Johnny; he'd have to look for him once he arrived. He never had any trouble locating his son, though. Even without being a plantation owner, Johnny was one of the more prominent citizens of Albemarle, and once John arrived at the small settlement, all he needed to do was ask anyone he saw about his son. The first person he asked said Johnny could be found with a group of men at the governor's house.

William Drummond, the new governor of Albemarle, was a character himself. He had risen to power after being an indentured servant upon his arrival in Virginia. He served an extra year in servitude for helping some other servants escape, but following that, he turned his life around. Over the last two decades and under the guidance of Berkeley, Drummond had become a justice of the peace and eventually the high sheriff of James City County. Berkeley was convinced he could control Drummond and maintain the running of the southern colony to his liking, so when the Lords Proprietors asked Berkeley for a recommendation to serve as the governor of Albemarle, Berkeley had recommended Drummond.

John walked down the dusty road toward the governor's house, passing wandering chickens who were pecking for morsels in the dirt. The last time John had been in Albemarle, it was to congratulate Samuel Stephens on his appointment as governor. John remembered being so proud of Frances and her husband. At the time, their house was the largest in town, but the last few years had seen much building in the settlement. The governor's house was now flanked by a meeting house and a tavern. A few men smoking pipes sat on a bench in front of the meeting house and nodded at John as he passed. A drunkard sat slouched on the porch of the tavern, leaning against the porch post and nearly dozing off in the afternoon sun, ignoring anything happening around him.

John knocked on the green door of the whitewashed governor's house and was promptly greeted by an Indian woman dressed in maid's attire. "I'm looking for Johnny Culpepper and was told he was here with Governor Drummond."

"Yes, sir. Please come in."

Johnny came out from one of the rooms. "Father? Is that your voice I hear?"

John smiled at his curly headed son and shook his hand. Johnny had grown into a man with broad shoulders and a firm handshake, but John still saw in Johnny's eyes the boy his son used to be. He still had that sparkle of mischief, and John found it curious that his son was a grown man and that time had passed so quickly. "I came down to see how you're doing. You look happy and healthy."

Johnny hugged him. "Oh, I'm doing quite well, Father. We have a new governor here, if you haven't heard." Johnny gestured to Drummond, who had followed him from the parlor. "Father, this is Governor Drummond. Governor, this is my father, John Culpepper."

Drummond reached for John's hand. "I believe I know of Mr. Culpepper from my time in Jamestown, but I'm not sure if we've ever met."

John shook the governor's hand. "No, I don't believe we have, but I sat in on the appointment meetings with Berkeley before you were given your commission, so I feel like I know you well."

Johnny gestured toward the other room. "Come into the parlor and let us get you something to drink. Did you just get into town?"

John nodded and followed the men into the parlor. Two men about Johnny's age rose from their chairs as John entered.

"Father, these are my good friends George Durant and Valentine Bird. George has a place up on the Little River and ships tobacco up to New England. Val collects the taxes on said tobacco." He narrowed his eyes at Durant and chuckled.

Durant grimaced.

John didn't understand the communication between the two.

Johnny explained. "Berkeley recently raised the taxes on exported tobacco, but our new friend and governor isn't the slightest bit interested in anything to do with taxing tobacco. We don't want to end up with an economically depressed town like Jamestown. We've suggested Val only charge half the tax he's supposed to, and the governor has agreed to pretend not to notice." Johnny laughed.

"It's still enough tax if you ask me," Durant added, downing what little brandy remained in his glass.

"Well, I don't know much about Berkeley's tobacco tax, but it's a pleasure to meet you gentlemen," John said, shaking hands with Durant and Bird.

Drummond handed John a glass of brandy. "We need to come up with some way to make up that tobacco tax money, though. Berkeley is going to expect his cut of the tax monies before they're sent to the Lords Proprietors, so somebody is going to need to show receipts for the shipments. Sadly, I don't know if we can make this work with Berkeley breathing down our necks."

John nodded. "That's quite a predicament, Governor."

Drummond shrugged and walked back to his seat near the fireplace. "We'll figure it all out."

"So, what brings you all the way down here, Father?"

"The usual. Your mother complained that she hadn't heard from you in a while and sent me on a mission to find you."

"I know I should write to her more often, but we've been so busy down here," Johnny said.

"Yes, you should write her more, but truthfully, I was also happy to come down and get away from Jamestown for a bit. The assembly is passing too many taxes and the Indians are an increasing problem. I needed to get out of there and clear my head."

"We're not having much better luck down here," the governor said. "The Indians aren't quite as fierce, but Berkeley's taxes have everyone down here in an uproar, too."

CHAPTER 5

August 1674, Nathaniel Bacon

Nathaniel Bacon strutted down the gangplank like he was the king himself, his tall, lanky frame carrying an air of superiority and arrogance. His wavy brown hair rose from the top of his head like a rooster's comb, and his thin, pale face was graced by a wide mustache and a pointed goatee. The clamor of the raucous sailors on the dock didn't distract him. His wife trailing behind him didn't disturb him, either. He walked straight toward Will and Frances Berkeley, who waited for him at the end of the dock.

"Welcome to Jamestown, cousin," Berkeley said, reaching out to shake Bacon's hand.

"Thank you. It's good to be on dry land. I never thought we'd get here." He rolled his eyes.

"I trust your journey was uneventful. This

is my wife, Frances. I believe you two are cousins, also."

Bacon removed his hat and swept a gallant bow before her. "Lady Berkeley, I am pleased to make your acquaintance."

Frances hid her face behind her lacy fan. She pulled out the skirt of her ruby dress and gave him a slight curtsey. "The pleasure is mine, Mr. Bacon."

"How are we related?" Bacon asked her.

"I'm not sure, but my uncle, John Culpepper, said you are a cousin to us."

"Oh, the Culpeppers! Sure. I'm familiar with your uncle, and now that you mention it, I know who your father was also. My father told me tales of Colonel Culpepper's military service to the king and his untimely demise here in Virginia."

"It was a great loss to us all."

"I'm sure it was."

Nathaniel's wife walked up behind him and stayed respectfully back about three feet. She was a mousy little thing who looked more like a servant, dressed in what looked like a brown burlap potato sack, unlike her handsome husband who wore the finest tailored and embroidered waistcoat with a matching overcoat and breeches. The rich blue fabric suited the color of his eyes. Nathaniel didn't acknowledge his wife behind him, and Berkeley, who had never met her, didn't know what to say, so he focused on Bacon.

"So, are you here to stay, Nathaniel?"

"I believe so. A London court insisted I fraudulently sold a parcel of land and I tire of their incessant legal proceedings, so there's not much left for me in England. I've come to claim my fortune in the colonies. Tell me it's better here. Tell me a man isn't brought up on false charges in the great colony of Virginia."

Berkeley squared his shoulders with pride. "We strive to maintain a high degree of honesty and integrity around these parts."

"Good. Perhaps you can help me acquire some property here that I can call my own," Bacon said.

"I'm sure we can find something to your liking, being family and all. I know of a tract of land in Henrico County, just northwest of here, that's for sale. And I'm certain I can create a substantial land grant to see that you're comfortable."

"I would appreciate that very kindly, cousin. For now, is it possible to stay with you until that happens?"

Berkeley glanced at Frances. Of course they had plenty of room at Green Spring, but they had assumed Bacon and his wife would be staying at the boarding house in Jamestown. Upon observing the man, they both realized he would never reside somewhere as common as a boarding house. "Of course you can stay with us at Green Spring. It's not far from the property I told you about, so we can go look at it as soon as you're rested from your journey."

"That sounds like a splendid plan. Shall we go?" Bacon waited for Berkeley to lead the way, never once acknowledging the quiet woman behind him or the young boys carting trunk after trunk off the ship. The wooden boxes were piled waist high in four heaps.

Berkeley glanced at the trunks and saw Frances do the same. "I'll…um…send someone for your belongings."

Bacon nodded, obviously not expecting anything less.

For the next few months, Bacon and his wife resided at Green Spring while they waited for the grant to go through on their new land. By the end of the third month, Frances was growing weary of the pompousness of her guests and was quite anxious to get the visitors out of her house. She insisted her husband offer Bacon a seat on the Virginia council, if only to get him out of the house for a little while so Frances could have a little peace and quiet. As the fall and winter dragged on, while Bacon built a mansion on his new land, Berkeley and Frances treated them as royalty, showering them with wine and spirits, feeding them the best Green Spring Plantation had to offer. Finally, after ten long months, when the first of the spring flowers began to bloom, Bacon and his wife, who it turns out was named Elizabeth, moved into their own house.

That spring saw the worst weather anyone in the colony could remember. Drought delayed planting. Hailstorms damaged property. Hurricanes and subsequent flooding washed away the newly planted crops, and what little crops survived the weather were destroyed during the continuing Indian attacks. Most planters were driven close to starvation, and there were more deaths of children that spring than at any other time in the history of Virginia. Many farmers were only months or weeks away from losing their land to Lord Thomas.

More and more residents attended Jamestown's council meetings, packing the state house with the stench of hot frustration and humid bodies. Some begged for food at the front door. Most pleaded with the governor to do something about the taxes and the Indians. Some even commanded he do something about the weather.

CHAPTER 6

July 1675, Doeg Indians

As summer heated the countryside with scorching temperatures, the struggles between the colonists and the Indians escalated. The Iroquois were at war with other tribes and the colonists were often caught in the crossfire. In one of the bloodiest battles, more than five hundred Iroquois were killed, and a larger number of colonists were slaughtered. As usual, the colonists received no assistance from their governor or their corrupt Virginia council.

In July, a month that saw temperatures repeatedly hit one hundred degrees, a trade deal went sour between some Doeg Indians and a plantation owner named Thomas Mathews, a neighbor of Nathaniel Bacon's. Upset over nonpayment, the Doeg Indians raided Mathews's plantation in the middle of the night.

Mathews, Bacon, and other neighbors chased and killed several of the Indians. The situation would have probably remained contained between the small group of men, but some colonists in Jamestown heard about the attack. Word quickly spread, and the colonists took matters into their own hands.

Two weeks after the Indian raid on his plantation, Thomas Mathews stood at the end of the rectangular table in the dining room of Nathaniel Bacon's home. "We have to do something about this situation. Berkeley's not going to help us. Our women and children are being killed in the crossfire. These Indians must be stopped."

The other dozen men in attendance mumbled and nodded.

"What do you gentlemen suggest we do?" Bacon asked.

"We need to kill all the Indians, and to do so, we need to form our own militia," one of the men said.

"Yes, we need to organize our men and fight off the Indians ourselves," another added.

Mathews interrupted them. "We all know what needs to be done." He turned to Bacon. "That's not the reason we've gathered. We're here to decide who is going to lead us."

By the end of the conversation, with wine flowing like water, the men had decided Bacon would lead the militia. While Bacon was flattered, he didn't want to antagonize the governor, who had granted him so much favor since his arrival. "You men understand that will be usurping the military prerogative of the governor?" Bacon asked.

"Of course we understand that," Mathews said. "But if Berkeley won't help us, we really have no choice."

The men left the meeting after Bacon promised them he'd think about it. For the moment, the militia would be formed with no leadership.

A few days later, the group formed a posse, loaded their guns, and set out with the intent of finding the remaining Doeg Indians.

* * *

Someone privy to both sides of the situation informed Berkeley of the forming militia. Berkeley immediately sent for John for advice.

"I know I've been unsuccessful in bringing the Indian situation under control, and I feel horrible about the loss of life due to my failure," Berkeley said from behind his desk in his office. He was tapping his chin.

John clenched his teeth at Berkeley's annoying tic, but he didn't want to bring it up at this time. He tempered his tone. "That's very kind of you, Will, but feeling bad doesn't correct the situation. You need to find a way to put an end to these Indian raids."

"But how am I supposed to do that when I can't raise an army?" Tap, tap, tap.

"Why is it the planters can raise a militia and you can't?

"I've been asking myself the same question."

"I think you need to talk to the planters and find out exactly what's going on. I don't believe all these raids are unprovoked."

"Will you go speak to them?" The tapping grew faster.

"Sure, I'd be happy to, but I think you need to speak with the tribal chiefs also. Some sort of agreement needs to be reached."

"All right, speak to the planters and let me know what they say, then we'll decide what to do next."

Three days later, John returned to Berkeley's office with news from the planters. "There have been a couple of skirmishes that were misunderstandings between the planters and the Indians, but according to the planters, most of the Indian engagements were motiveless, malicious attacks. The Indians are simply being the savages they are. They don't know any better."

"What am I supposed to do about them?

They don't consider themselves under my rule. I can't just pass a new law to make them behave."

John drummed his fingers on the table and thought for a moment. "Is it possible to speak with the tribal chiefs directly?"

"I assume so. Would you be willing to speak with them?"

"No, I'm sorry, Will. It isn't my place."

Berkeley raised his hand to his chin and John turned away and looked out the window. After a moment, Berkeley spoke. "Then I guess we should hold a meeting. We will let the colonists and the tribal chiefs speak directly."

"Will you lead the meeting?"

"No, no, I don't want to get involved, either. The colonists already think I favor the Indians by trading with them, and if I make the Indians angry, they'll take it out on the colonists, not to mention stop trading with us. If they're angered, the raids will increase, and the colonists will think it my fault. No, I don't think I should even be there." After a moment, he added, "Bacon seems to be itching to do something important. I'll let him lead the meeting."

* * *

Before word reached Bacon about the suggested meeting, Bacon and his men set out to the Doeg village. They hiked through the forest of red maple and locust trees and cautiously entered the center of the village, their weapons at the ready. It was quiet, with only the occasional chirp of songbirds in the trees. Bacon and his posse stood in the center of the village square, looking around and listening. The village was empty. The Indian men were often off hunting, but Bacon expected at least women and children to be loitering about. Mathews led the way, walking between houses called yehakins that were built in a circle surrounding the village square. They were dome-like structures made of saplings and covered with large mats made from marsh reeds. On one edge of the circle stood sturdy frames holding rows and rows of animal hides—deer, beaver, raccoon. On the other side of the circle sat drying pottery. The ornate bowls and vases depicted scenes of hunts and pictures of animals, surrounded by geometric designs bordering the tops and bottoms. A small fire glowed in the middle of the clearing, sending gray puffs of smoke skyward, but it was low and probably hadn't been tended for at least an hour or two.

"Where do you think everyone went?" Mathews asked Bacon.

Bacon shrugged.

As they began to put their weapons away, a loud war whoop came from the tree. An arrow went through Mathews's arm, spinning him around. He fell onto the pile of pottery, smashing it. Bacon ducked behind one of the yehakins, and the other men followed suit. They fired their weapons into the woods. Arrows flew back in return. The battle continued for nearly two hours.

* * *

The next morning, John stood in Berkeley's office. Berkeley sat behind his desk, stirring his hot cider with a spoon.

"Will, are you listening? It was a massacre!"

"I'm sure *massacre* is a strong word, but the Indians are gone now, right?" Berkeley blew into his cup.

"You don't understand. Bacon's men killed every man, woman, and child in the Indian village."

"Well, it's a shame it had to come to this, but what's wrong with that?"

"They went to attack the Doeg in retaliation for the attack on Mathews's plantation, but they must have gotten turned around on their way to the village. They attacked the wrong tribe."

Berkeley looked at John, his eyes large. "The wrong tribe?"

"Yes. It's a tragic incident."

"If what you say is true, this will only cause the Indian raids to increase."

"That's what I'm trying to tell you. You

need to set up that meeting immediately."

* * *

The following week, the Susquehanna, Iroquois, Appomattox, and Maryland Indians met at the state house with Bacon, Mathews, and various members of the council. The meeting began as a promising collaboration between the Indians and the men of the colony, but as word of the gathering spread on the street, angry and violent planters descended upon the state house, and the conference ended in bloody disaster. A melee ensued, and when all was said and done, several of the Indian chiefs had been murdered.

In the months that followed, Berkeley pleaded for restraint from his people, but the colonists ignored his orders to not harm the Indians. Planters seized and hung some friendly Appomattox Indians for allegedly stealing corn from one of the colonists.

Berkeley called the responsible parties forward and reprimanded them for the hangings, placing them in the stocks in front of the state house. This action caused confusion and anger in the colony. Why would Berkeley support the Indians? Why would he reprimand his own citizens for standing up against the savages? Rumors quickly spread that Berkeley was an Indian supporter. After all, he and his rich cronies profited most from trading with them.

A second meeting was held at Bacon's house. Mathews, again, stood at the head of the table. This time, his arm was wrapped in a bandage. A small amount of blood seeped through the white material, spotting it with dark red color.

"Nathaniel, I am going to ask you again to lead our militia," Mathews said.

Bacon took a deep breath as his thoughts spun round and round. An organized militia would be illegal and could be construed as treasonous. It could be a hanging offense. Yet, if they didn't form one, they stood to lose everything. The Indians raids were becoming more frequent and more deadly. Bacon looked around the room at the men who were anxiously awaiting his decision. He had to admit he had begun enjoying his newfound popularity. He had recently decided he would be happy as the head of the militia, especially since Berkeley seemed to be blundering the situation. If Bacon played his cards right, he could run his bumbling cousin out of office and become the governor of Virginia. Berkeley seemed to have everything—money, prestige, respect. Bacon would enjoy having those things that seemed to come with the title of governor.

After Bacon distributed a large quantity of brandy, a vote was taken and he was unanimously elected the militia leader.

CHAPTER 7

Maryland Indians

In retaliation for the hanging of the Appomattox Indians, a band of Maryland Indians sneaked into a small town on the outskirts of Jamestown. They crossed the Potomac on a Sunday morning as the sun rose, and waited in the trees surrounding the village. There were about twenty homes built on two parallel streets. Once the families left to attend church at the end of one of the streets, the Indians set all the homes ablaze.

At the small church, as the pastor offered his closing prayer, a man ran in screaming, "Fire! Fire! There's smoke everywhere!"

The pastor stopped speaking and everyone turned to the man.

"Smoke from at least a dozen houses!" The man pointed outside.

The churchgoers ran to the door and

struggled to get outside, pushing each other out of the way. When they emerged onto the street, they saw massive plumes of black smoke billowing into the sky from the direction of their homes. Confusion and panic broke out. Some men took off running, yelling for their wives and children to remain safely at the church. Some sprinted toward their wagons, yelling for their families to hurry. Horses whinnied and bucked. The long skirts of the women dragging on the ground caused a cloud of dust to encircle the chaos.

It had been a parched fall with no rain whatsoever in the last two weeks, so there was little water in the rain barrels. Most of the wooden homes burned quickly to the ground. Only a few made of stone could be salvaged. On the far edge of town, some men caught sight of the Indians and pursued them. At the end of the day, eighteen houses were heaps of charred rubble and two of the town's residents had been killed by the Indians.

That evening, the militia again converged on Nathaniel Bacon's house to discuss retaliation. John Culpepper joined them.

"We need to hunt down these savage Indians," one man said. "Their violence is increasing and it's not safe here as long as they're in the woods."

John watched all of the men roar in agreement. *What are these men suggesting? That they kill every Indian?* John was shocked that the men were in such a state of rage. The life of every man in attendance had nearly been destroyed by the Indians, either financially or by the death of a loved one or the threat of starvation and homelessness. There was unanimous and hearty agreement that the colonists needed to come up with a plan — a plan of slaughter. John knew voicing his concerns would be futile. He watched and remained silent as the men continued their frenzied conversation deep into the night.

Without a word to any of the men, John left Bacon's house and rode through the darkness as fast as his horse would run. He barged into Berkeley's house without knocking. The lamps were lit, so John knew someone in the house was still awake.

"Will! Will, where are you? It's an emergency," John called.

Berkeley stepped out of the dining room, a napkin tucked in his collar, a large turkey leg in his hand. "John? What's wrong?"

"Bacon and his men are going to kill the Maryland Indians!"

"Oh, they've been threatening that for months," he said as he turned and headed back into the dining room. He gestured for John to follow him. "Come. Have something to eat. I'm having a little midnight snack."

John followed him. "No, you don't

understand. The Indians set fire to more than a dozen homes yesterday, and two colonists were killed in the pursuit of the arsonists."

"I heard something about that. I was going to take a ride out there tomorrow morning and have a look-see."

"Tomorrow may be too late. A few hours ago, the men were roaring about going to kill the Indians—all of the Indians!"

"They're only going to make matters worse. Don't they realize there are more Indians than they could ever kill? And not all Indians are savages. We trade with some of them." Berkeley sat down at the head of the table. He removed his napkin from his chest, wiped his mouth, and dropped the napkin onto the table with a sigh. "Are you sure you don't want something to eat?"

John shook his head.

"I think the more pressing issue is, what are we going to do about Bacon?" Berkeley said.

"Who cares about Bacon? We need to stop these men from slaughtering the Indians."

"They wouldn't slaughter anyone if Bacon wasn't goading them into doing so. I've heard he's been overstepping his authority. He pretends he's the head of a mighty militia, but I gave him no such charge. How he could raise any kind of militia in this town is beyond me. I've been trying to do so for years."

By the time Berkeley and John had

finished their discussion without reaching a conclusion about what to do, the sun was shining through the dining room windows, and Bacon's men had already ridden into the Indian village and killed ten Maryland Indian braves and their chief.

CHAPTER 8

January 1676, Susquehanna Indians

The weather was unusually warm and the blanket of snow that had previously covered the roads and fields had melted, turning the ground into a spongy, muddy mess. The sky was clear and the moon had long since disappeared behind the horizon, leaving the night black. A group of Occaneechi Indians tiptoed into Jamestown, quiet as deer, nearly invisible. In the market square, they passed shops, the church, the state house. They were on a mission of revenge, having had enough of white men killing their friends and destroying their lives.

Without a war whoop from the lead warrior, the Indians silently broke into the dwellings of the residents. One would expect screams to overtake the predawn silence, but the Indians moved with stealth and speed. They

began doing what they came into town to do —
leave a path of death and destruction, a trail so
lethal, the white men would cower and never
raise arms to the Indians again. When the first
colonial gunshot rang out, the Indians
disappeared into the night just as quickly and
silently as they had appeared.

The sun began to rise amidst sobs and
wails as residents discovered the extent of the
massacre. Thirty-six colonists had lost their lives
in the wee hours of the morning. They lay in
their beds, covered with blood, knife and hatchet
wounds on their necks and chests.

Later that day, Berkeley summoned his
cabinet to an emergency meeting at the state
house to discuss the Indian situation. As they sat
in his office, residents barged into the meeting,
demanding retaliation.

"I beg you to use some restraint and
caution. You can't keep going after them,"
Berkeley said to the angry crowd. "They are
going to gather more braves and come back with
a vengeance. We don't have the manpower here
in Jamestown to keep them at bay."

One man stepped forward. "Governor,
with all due respect, my wife and both of my
sons were killed in the raid last night. I'm not
going to sit here and listen to your excuses any
longer. We need to form a search party and find
these dirty savages and do away with them. I
don't understand why you are so unwilling to

help us. I heard Nathaniel Bacon has organized a militia against the Indians. I think we should follow Mr. Bacon's example."

"No, no, no, don't follow Bacon. He is acting against my express wishes to keep the peace. An eye for an eye is not the way to solve this problem. It will only create more complications and more bloodshed."

"Then what are you going to do for us, Governor?" a farmer asked.

Berkeley sighed. "The only thing I can do at this time is to call for new elections to the House of Burgesses. The members of the House who are currently in charge are obviously not doing their jobs. We need more reliable men in their position to better facilitate this Indian problem."

"Indian problem?" the farmer asked sarcastically.

Berkeley looked at the farmer, and over the farmer's shoulder, he saw John enter and stand against the wall, his face pale. Berkeley wanted to ask him for help, he wanted John to come up with a solution, to settle the crowd, to put an end to this Indian situation, but John didn't approach him. Berkeley tapped his chin.

"Is that what you're calling this violent and senseless act of murder, Governor? An Indian problem?" the farmer continued.

Tap, tap, tap.

Meanwhile, at Nathaniel Bacon's house, a group of men gathered to discuss retaliation for the massacre in Jamestown. The new militia gathered their weapons and food stores to last a few days, and journeyed south to the land of the Susquehannock. They negotiated with the Susquehanna to attack the Occaneechi village in their stead. They offered the Susquehanna weapons, powder, and shot if they would run the Occaneechi away, or better yet, kill them all.

The Susquehanna did as they were asked. They massacred the entire Occaneechi village.

Following the bloody encounter, Bacon and his men returned to the Susquehannock village to pay their debt.

According to colonial records, more than five thousand Susquehanna were living in Virginia in 1600. By the 1630s, that number had dwindled to three hundred. Today, there couldn't be more than thirty.

Instead of giving the tribe what was promised, Bacon's men set out killing all of the tribe—men, women, and children. The Susquehanna were annihilated.

CHAPTER 9

Drummond Resigns

Governor Drummond's tenure in Albemarle was supposed to have lasted only two years. After not being able to get Berkeley to send a replacement or even respond to his letters as of late, Drummond abandoned Albemarle at the end of the third year. Discouraged by Berkeley's unfulfilled promises to send a replacement and disheartened with Berkeley himself, Drummond returned to his home in Jamestown, Virginia. His wife, Sarah, was pleased.

John knocked on the door of the large house and was greeted by Sarah Drummond.

"You must be Mr. Culpepper." She smiled warmly and escorted him into the lush parlor.

Drummond rose from the red settee to greet him. "Mr. Culpepper! I'm so glad you came. Your son escorted me from Albemarle and was anxious to get word to you that he was in town."

"Is he here?" John looked around the room.

"He'll be back shortly. I asked him to go down the road and invite my friend Richard Lawrence to supper. Won't you please stay and dine with us?"

"It would be my pleasure. When did you get here?"

"The day before yesterday. I don't know if Berkeley has heard yet."

"Oh, he's heard all right. He's quite upset with you."

"He's upset with me? I've been upset with him for an entire year. I've been stuck in Albemarle without my family for three years, and I couldn't even get Berkeley to respond to my letters. I was supposed to be home a year ago."

"I understand your frustration, Mr. Drummond, and I know sometimes Berkeley is slow to respond. I deal with him on a daily basis."

They heard the front door open and shut. Within moments, Johnny came around the corner. He grinned when he saw his father standing in the room.

"Father! I'm so glad you got my message."

John hugged his son. "I certainly did. How long will you be in town? You know your mother will want to see you."

"I'm afraid I won't be here long." He glanced at Drummond. "Somebody needs to see to Albemarle. We recently lost our governor, if you haven't heard."

John smiled at the sarcasm. "Yes, I heard."

Johnny continued. "Well, my friends who you met when you came down, George Durant and Valentine Bird, are struggling to keep things orderly down there until the Lords Proprietors or Berkeley sends a new governor. I need to be there to help them."

John patted him on the shoulder. "I'm glad to see you standing up to your civic responsibilities."

Johnny shook his head. "I don't know about all that, Father. I just don't want the Indians or the transient merchants stealing my things or destroying my town."

John smiled.

"Is Mr. Lawrence coming for supper?" Sarah interrupted.

"Yes. He's right behind me and will be here in a few minutes."

"Good. I'll set the table for one more and we'll eat as soon as he arrives."

When Richard Lawrence arrived, the group sat down for supper and the conversation quickly turned to Berkeley's complete and total incompetence.

"Why can't Berkeley form a militia when Bacon seems to have no trouble at all forming one?" Sarah asked.

"That's probably nothing you need to concern yourself over, my dear," her husband answered.

"It is a good question, though," Johnny said. "Father, perhaps you know the answer."

They all turned to John.

John placed his wine glass on the table and cleared his throat, a bit surprised at being put on the spot. "I'm afraid Berkeley hasn't been making many friends these days. He has taxed Virginians until they're almost in the poorhouse. Bacon came to town with his youthful energy, and everyone has jumped at the chance to follow him. As usual, in the absence of leadership, the masses will follow anyone with the slightest inkling of what needs to be done."

"Perhaps we should make Bacon the new governor," Lawrence said.

John looked at Lawrence with disbelief. They had never met, but John knew of Lawrence and heard he was a strong supporter of Bacon's militia and was widely known as an anti-berkeleyan. But Bacon as governor? Surely he was joking.

Drummond cleared his throat. "Perhaps we should send Bacon down to Albemarle. I hear they're looking for a governor."

Sarah laughed at her husband's joke.

"That would make Berkeley very happy," John said under his breath.

The room silenced as everyone waited for John to continue. He looked from face to face and thought there would no harm in stating his opinion in this circle. "Berkeley is very unhappy with Bacon. I think if Bacon doesn't curb his enthusiasm for gathering men and killing Indians, Berkeley will soon declare him a rebel."

"Do you think he's a rebel, Father?"

John shrugged. "I think he's ambitious."

Drummond, Lawrence, and Johnny glanced at one another. John didn't know what these men were up to, but he wished his son wouldn't get involved. He would have to speak with him in private later.

A few days after the gathering, John sent word for Johnny to come to Accomac to see his mother, but Johnny had already left to return to Albemarle.

CHAPTER 10

Indians and News Wives

In March 1676, Berkeley called together his assembly and officially declared war on all "bad" Indians. The first order of business was to form a paid army to protect Jamestown, and in order to pay this army, taxes were raised. The assembly also demanded that colonists cut all ties with the Indians, even if they had been trading with them for generations. Of course, Berkeley and his friends were exempt from this ban. The assembly formed a commission to monitor trading among those who were allowed to do so, and make sure the Indians did not receive any guns or ammunition.

"Will, it looks to the colonists like you're favoring the Indians," John said.

"No, I'm not favoring them. I just want to make sure the Indians don't get their hands on our guns."

"You and your friends can trade with the Indians, but the colonists are banned from doing so? It doesn't look good. Once again, the residents of Virginia are being financially injured by your laws but your friends are protected. You have to stop doing this. It's just making more and more people angry."

"I'm protecting the colonists. If the Indians get their hands on English weapons, the residents will only be in more danger. Don't they see? I'm guarding their welfare. Surely, they have to understand that."

"They don't. I don't, either. You can say anything you want about their welfare, but word is spreading like wildfire that you're playing favorites. You're displaying cronyism to your friends and protecting the Indians, but you're neglecting your people. Bacon has openly accused you of such and word is spreading quickly."

"Bacon?" Berkeley shook his head and sighed. "I'm so tired of Nathaniel Bacon and his antics. Maybe I should speak to him in person and get this all sorted out. Would you travel out to his house and invite him to Green Spring to discuss the matter? If we sit down and have a conversation, perhaps we can put this to rest once and for all."

Two days later, Bacon strutted into

Berkeley's house as if he owned the place. His heels pounded on the wooden floors as he stomped into the dining room without being led by a servant. Berkeley and John sat quietly in the room, enjoying cups of hot cider as they awaited their breakfast. After being ignored by Berkeley for a few moments, Bacon tossed his hat on the dining table and cleared his throat.

Berkeley didn't look up and didn't rise from his chair. "Nathaniel, have a seat."

Bacon sat down, glanced at John and back at Berkeley. His jaw twitched as he clenched his teeth.

"Cousin, I'm afraid we're having some communication issues, so I wanted to meet with you and sort them out."

"What sort of issues would you be referring to?" Bacon's body was tense, his eyes narrowed.

"Well, I hear that you've taken issue with the ban on trading with the Indians."

"I have."

"What's the problem? We need to make sure the Indians are not being armed."

"I agree with that statement, but I don't see how allowing your friends to trade with them will assure that. Your rich friends are the only ones capable of giving the Indians any weapons. Poor farmers can't do that. They don't have the means of giving away weapons no matter what the Indians offered in return."

"My friends are not going to arm the savages, and you, being a member of the council, agreed to the legislation."

"I never agreed to it. I was one of those who opposed. It's absurd. The farmers will be hurt by the lack of trade, and how do you know your corrupt friends aren't going to arm the Indians?"

Berkeley huffed. "I know them."

"So, your knowing someone, no matter how mistaken you might be, is grounds for passing legislature?"

"That is illogical. I passed the law to protect the people of Jamestown."

"No, you passed yet another law that tied their hands even further. They're being taxed to death. You've demanded they not fight off the Indians, and now you've given the Indians all the power to make an income but have taken away free trade from your own people."

"It does sound harsh when you put it that way, but I assure you, I'm only doing what's best for the citizens of Virginia."

"If you want to do what's best, then grant me a commission as leader of the militia. I'll see to the Indians."

Berkeley coughed. "No, no, I couldn't do that. You are far too hot tempered for the job. We need someone more, how shall I put it, more levelheaded."

"Levelheaded?" Bacon blew a swish of air

through his teeth. "If you won't grant me the commission, then I must ask you to send your militia to retaliate in the murder of my neighbor's overseer and three of his servants. We believe it was the Pamunkeys who did it. Your paid army didn't keep my neighbor's property safe, and if they don't come now in retaliation, they are useless."

"What did your neighbor do to attract this behavior from the Pamunkeys?" John asked.

"He did nothing." Bacon looked from John to Berkeley. "Nothing!" he said again. "The savages attacked because that's what they do. We need the help of the government and this paid militia you are forming, and I'm asking you to send your men."

"No, I'm afraid I cannot convene an army for one person's revenge."

"So, you won't send your army to help?"

"No, I won't."

"And you refuse to make me the head of the militia?"

"That's correct."

"Then our discussion is finished." Bacon rose and stomped from the room. The next sound Berkeley and John heard was the slamming of the front door.

Berkeley didn't call after him. He rang the little bell on the corner of the table and a servant girl entered the room.

"Yes, m'lord." She curtsied.

"Bring me some breakfast, girl."

"Yes, m'lord."

John frowned at Berkeley, wondering if his oldest and dearest friend had indeed lost his mind. It was obvious from Bacon's past performance and angry demeanor this morning that he meant business. John had a suspicion Bacon would be more trouble to Berkeley than the Indians had ever been.

When Bacon returned home, he found the neighbor with the murdered overseer waiting on his doorstep.

"What did Berkeley say?" the man asked.

"He refused to help. It looks like the only thing we can do is fight the Indians off ourselves. But, of course, we already knew that. Gather the men and tell them to arrive well-armed. First thing in the morning, we'll drive the Pamunkeys off the nearby land, and we'll kill every one of them we come across. We'll leave a trail of blood all the way to the West. That'll send a message to all Indians that we will no longer tolerate their savage actions."

Following the raid on the Pamunkeys, Berkeley issued two petitions. The first declared Bacon a rebel and relieved him of the council seat he had been given. The second was to offer a pardon to any of Bacon's men who returned home peacefully.

Though Berkeley would not send his men to retaliate for an Indian attack, he sent three hundred men to Henrico County to flush Bacon out and bring him in. Berkeley understood Bacon was well loved in the community, so in an attempt to maintain peace in the colony, Berkeley stood on the steps of the state house and publicly declared he would see to it that Bacon received a fair trial once he was brought in.

When Bacon got word Berkeley's men were on their way, he fled into the forest with two hundred of his own men. But instead of lying low and going into hiding, Bacon ramped up his efforts to eliminate the Indians and destroy Berkeley. His group attacked the Occaneechi camp on the Roanoke River and stole its store of beaver pelts.

A few days after the Occaneechi attack, Berkeley met with John at his office in Jamestown.

"What are we going to do about Bacon?" Berkeley asked.

"We? You shouldn't have made him an enemy. The people love him."

"He's an arrogant son of a bitch."

"That may be, but he's not the one

burdening the people with all these taxes. He's not the one taking away their free trade. He's the one giving them what they want — retaliation against these Indian attacks. He's becoming a hero around here."

"Hero?" Berkeley groaned.

"Perhaps you should reconsider and grant him the commission as head of the militia."

"I can't make him the head of the militia, especially now that I've declared him a rebel."

John sighed and ran his fingers through his graying curls. He narrowed his eyes at Berkeley.

"What is it?" Berkeley asked.

"I'm afraid you have a new problem now."

"What?"

"Bacon has enlisted the help of the women."

"What women? What could women possible do?"

John shook his head at his friend's ignorance. "I would think you'd know by simply being married to Frances that women run this colony. They do so behind closed doors, in sewing circles, at the market square, in their church groups. Bacon's wife has become good friends with Mrs. Grindon, Mrs. Lloyd, Mrs. Stag, and Mrs. Cheezeman, and they're spreading Bacon's propaganda. They're referring to you as an Indian lover."

"Indian lover?" Berkeley repeated with a snarl. "Oh, that's absurd. Who in their right mind would believe something like that?"

"Apparently everyone. The people of Jamestown are struggling to feed and clothe their families, and all they understand from you is that they should keep quiet or you'll raise their taxes even higher. The women are spreading the word that you're a better friend to the Indians than to the English."

"They sound like a bunch of chickens cackling in the yard."

"They're not just cackling, Will. They're delivering the news people want to hear."

"News. Bacon's lies and propaganda aren't news."

"In lieu of hearing anything else, the people believe what they're told."

"Well, these news wives had better watch themselves."

"Are you threatening the women now?"

Berkeley sighed and looked down at his desk. He propped his elbow on the edge of the desk and began tapping on his chin. "No, I'm not threatening women." He looked up at John. "Who is their leader—Mrs. Bacon?"

John shook his head. "Sarah Drummond."

"Sarah Drummond? William Drummond's wife? Oh, my goodness. This just gets better and better. Drummond has had it out for me since he resigned as governor of Albemarle, leaving me in a bind, I might add. He said I left him down there and didn't return his letters. He also accused me of some bad land deals down there, but his accusations are completely unfounded."

John nodded, knowing well the Albemarle situation. "Apparently Mrs. Drummond is telling everyone that the Virginia tax dollars you've collected are unaccounted for, and that you're keeping a sizeable amount of money for yourself. She said you're raising six thousand sterling per year in taxes, but are only spending one thousand on the colony. She has people now questioning how you're using the other five thousand. All this is on top of your alleged love for the Indians."

Berkeley rose, walked to the window, and looked out at the town square, his hands clasped behind his back. "What happened here, John? I used to be respected by the people."

"Times change. Maybe it's time to consider stepping down."

"Perhaps you're right. I could ask the king to appoint a suitable successor and tell everyone I will resign as soon as my replacement arrives."

"Do you think the masses would quiet if you did that?"

"I don't know, but if the king were to appoint someone like Bacon, then all is lost. The colony can't survive someone like him. If I were to resign, I would need to go to England and speak directly with the king. He needs to understand what's happening here and what's at stake, but I can't leave right now with the colony in such a state. Maybe you would go?"

"No, I'm not sailing to England. I'm much too old to spend two months on a ship. I promised myself I wouldn't sail again unless it was a family emergency."

"You don't consider this a family emergency?"

"I'm sure you can find someone else. Maybe Frances would go. She'd probably love to visit her brother while she's there."

"Perhaps," Berkeley mumbled.

"Not to add more wood to this fire, but I heard that your friends, whom you've allowed to trade with the Indians, gave them powder, shot, and guns. Rumor is that the Indians are now armed."

Berkeley dropped his head and closed his eyes. He exhaled a long draft of air. He sat back down at his desk and began his infernal tapping.

CHAPTER 11

Berkeley's Retreat

In the brightness of the morning sun, a young boy in a floppy, brown hat pounded a nail into a stiff piece of paper onto the front door of the state house. Townspeople in the market square meandered and watched until the boy finished hammering, then they hurried over to see what the announcement had to say. Jockeying for position and looking over each other's heads, they found it was a declaration by Governor Berkeley to the people of Jamestown. It stated his great love for the colony of Virginia and its beloved residents, listing the numerous acts of his distinguished service for ten years under King Charles I and for sixteen years under King Charles II. It concluded by repeating that no one loved or served the colony more loyally than Berkeley. Word of the declaration spread like fire through Jamestown, with the colonists question its intent. Some thought it an honest gesture. Some thought it a political maneuver.

Hours later, while the town murmured over the declaration, Berkeley placed his treasury of gold and silver plate from Green Spring on board a carriage and sent it and his wife to John's house. Once Frances and their life savings were safely out of town, Berkeley called for his sergeant at arms.

"Yes, Governor." The man stood like a pillar of stone in the dining room at Green Spring.

"I want you to gather some men and find Bacon and arrest him."

"How many men?"

Berkeley scratched his head. "This man is as slippery as a fish. I think you'll need a lot of men."

"Dozens?" the man asked.

"More."

"More?"

Berkeley nodded. "Hundreds. I don't want him to escape this time, and there's a possibility you'll have to fight through his illegal militia to get to him."

"Should we engage them or try a diplomatic approach, sir?"

"Engage them. Kill them all if you have to. I want Bacon captured!" Berkeley rose from his chair and his voice rose loudly enough to be heard at the end of Sugar Row. "I want Bacon in jail immediately! I want his head on a platter for the damage he's done to the colony and to my reputation! I want to see him hanged!"

"Yes, sir. I'll organize the men immediately."

After the man left the house, Berkeley went upstairs and began placing some clothing in a satchel.

"Sir?" one of the maids entered the bedchambers.

"Yes." He didn't turn around.

"Are you going somewhere, sir?"

"Yes."

"Will you be joining Lady Berkeley?"

"Yes."

"When will you be returning, sir?"

"I don't know."

Without another word, Berkeley left Green Spring and took the back roads, avoiding Jamestown at all costs. He rode alone, traveling to join Frances in Accomac.

CHAPTER 12

Bacon's Sloop

Since Berkeley hadn't been seen for the last month and no one knew his whereabouts, Bacon figured this was his opportunity to make his presence known as a viable alternative for governor. He had spent the last four weeks outrunning Berkeley's sergeant at arms, being told of each and every move Berkeley's men made, thanks to the loyal army of supporters he had amassed. He promised the people of Virginia he would protect them from the Indians, and so far, he had fulfilled that promise. He had also enjoyed commanding his own militia and had a growing desire to run the colony. In the absence of the true governor who had run away like a frightened child, now was the time to convince the members of the assembly to stand behind him. He thought he had a good chance of fulfilling his wishes. Once he appeared at the state house and indicated his desires, the council members would surely run Berkeley out of office. They would petition the king in Bacon's favor, naming the many times and ways he had protected the colony, and the citizens would support him, just as they had in becoming the general of the militia. They were tired of Berkeley's oppression and taxation. They saw Bacon as their savior, their deliverer. He knew the people would support his bid for governor. He was certain of it. But first, he needed to regain his seat in the council.

His newly-purchased sloop wound its way down the James River and dropped anchor across from Jamestown. On board, his crew and forty bodyguards were prepared for the best and the worst. Bacon didn't know how the assembly would react to his unannounced appearance at the state house. He commanded some of his crew to row over and ask the assembly if it would be safe for him to take his seat among them. He watched quietly as they crossed the river. The seabirds cackled as Bacon remained on the deck, awaiting the return of his men with the council's answer. The noon sun began its westward descent, and Bacon still waited.

"Captain, I don't think they're coming back," said one of the sailors.

"They'll return. We just need to be patient."

"What could be taking them so long?

Surely they've received an answer by now."

"I know from experience that this assembly takes forever to make a decision, and I'm sure my men will be cautious and make sure the way is safe for me. They're good men. They will convince the assembly to allow me to come ashore, especially since Berkeley has flown the coop. The assembly needs someone to lead them, someone who understands their predicament and the plight of the colonists. It will work out in our favor. You'll see. Why wouldn't the council want me to come back? I'm probably the only one in Jamestown who can lead them through the loss of their governor."

While stating all this, Bacon silently wondered if the assembly *would* be favorable to his request. Would they allow him to take his seat, or try to arrest him per Berkeley's orders?

Suddenly there was a loud boom from the direction of Jamestown's Brick Fort, followed by the splash of a cannonball near the bow of Bacon's ship. That answered his question. A puff of smoke rose from Brick Fort, and a second boom sounded. The next cannonball hit the front of Bacon's ship, tearing a hole in her bow. Men scurried around, checking the damage. The third cannonball hit the ship's bulwark, ripping it like a piece of rotted cloth.

"Cut the anchor! Get us out of here before they sink us!" Bacon yelled to his men.

As cannonballs whirled around them,

some hitting the ship, some splashing into the water nearby, the crew cut the anchor's rope, raised the sails, and fled upstream. As they passed Sandy Bay, they were fired on again, this time from two ships near the shore. They kept moving upstream. Fortunately, the attacking ships stayed moored to the dock.

As night fell and no one appeared in pursuit, Bacon anchored his sloop further north, and with the first light of morning, he and his bodyguards disembarked and walked unmolested through a small fishing town. They entered the dense woods and headed toward Richard Lawrence's house.

With the recent Indian attacks, the lack of the promised forts, and the now missing governor, there would surely be talk of a rebellion against the assembly and the status quo. The members of the House were supposed to defend the people, but they had failed miserably. There was a good chance that Lawrence, being a staunch anti-berkeleyan, would have word of what was to come. Despite what happened yesterday in Jamestown, perhaps this *was* the time for Bacon to rise to power, if not as governor then as the leader of an anti-government rebellion.

Bacon entered Lawrence's house and was warmly greeted by Lawrence and William Drummond. "Gentlemen, it's good to see you."

"You didn't let anyone follow you, did

you?" Lawrence asked.

"Of course not. My men are patrolling the woods. No one from Berkeley's camp will get through."

"How many men do you have in the woods?" Drummond asked.

"About fifty, but there are over two hundred more nearby and awaiting my orders."

"We heard what happened in Jamestown yesterday. Did they do much damage to your ship?"

"Nearly sank her." He scanned the room and his eyes fell on a young man sitting at the far end in front of the fireplace.

Lawrence followed his line of sight and made the introduction. "Nathaniel Bacon, I'd like you to meet Johnny Culpepper. Johnny, this is Nathaniel Bacon."

Johnny rose to his feet and held out his hand in greeting. "Mr. Bacon, I've heard a lot about you."

"Culpepper? John Culpepper's son?"

Johnny vigorously shook Bacon's hand. "One and the same, sir."

The young man resembled his father, though he was more muscular. This must be what John Culpepper looked like in his youth, Bacon thought—a handsome rogue with a glint of mischief in his eyes. Johnny's smile was warm and genuine. Bacon judged him to be about thirty years old. His face was slightly weathered, but there were no wrinkles around his eyes and his hair held no hint of gray. "How did you get mixed up in this mess?"

"I've been by Mr. Drummond's side for a long time, sir. Berkeley, although a friend of my father's, has not been the most upstanding gentleman when it comes to matters of Carolina. His rulings were quite deceptive over some land grants down there. I haven't trusted him since."

"I'm certain your father would be sad to know you're on the rebel's side."

"My father isn't an issue here, Mr. Bacon. The corrupt Virginia assembly is the issue."

The entire day and night, the four men discussed the Indians, the council, and detailed plans for a massive rebellion, and as the sun rose, Bacon called in his men who were scattered in the nearby woods. To the beat of a drum, which had been previously planned as a summons, they returned to Bacon's ship.

They sailed quietly back down the James River without incident, but as they were about to clear the bay, a ship approached them — the *Adam & Eve* of London. The sheriff of James City County appeared on the deck and yelled across the empty space between the two ships.

"I have a warrant for the arrest of Nathaniel Bacon."

"We know of no such name," a sailor yelled.

"I know this is Bacon's ship. I know he is

aboard. I will give you five minutes to surrender him or I shall commence firing upon your ship."

No verbal response came from Bacon's men, but they scrambled, raising what was left of their tattered sails and loading their weapons. They wouldn't turn over their captain easily. They would fight, even with a damaged ship.

The *Adam & Eve*, newer and faster than Bacon's sloop, maneuvered her way in front of Bacon's ship and blocked her advance into the bay. To avoid a collision, Bacon's men were forced to drop the sails and stop dead in the water. The two ships sat quietly, waiting for the other to make the next move.

Finally, the sheriff yelled, "Five minutes is up."

The *Adam & Eve* fired at Bacon's sloop. The cannonball flew over the bow of the ship and hit the water only inches away. It didn't damage the ship, but it did get the sailors' attention.

"Drop your anchor!" the sheriff yelled.

Bacon's sailors reluctantly dropped the one anchor they had left.

Bacon sat below deck waiting for the sheriff and his men to board his ship, but time passed and they never tried to do so.

"They know we're armed," said Bacon to one of his men.

"But how long can we wait them out? They will fire again eventually. They will sink us, Captain."

"Let's wait and see what they do," Bacon said.

As afternoon turned to evening and evening to night, Bacon realized the *Adam & Eve* wasn't going anywhere. He decided it would be better to fight another day than to drown in the mouth of the Chesapeake Bay. He ordered his men to surrender.

Sixteen sailors and forty bodyguards walked onto the deck with their hands held in the air.

Two small boats approached the sloop and rowed the prisoners to shore in several trips, which took hours. The last to be rowed ashore was Bacon, held at gunpoint.

Once everyone was off Bacon's sloop, and Bacon was being held captive in a rowboat only a few yards away, he heard the sheriff yelled, "Sink it!"

Cannons exploded, blasting holes through the crippled ship, and within the hour, the sloop bubbled and faltered, disappearing from sight beneath the waters of the bay. As the last of the mast sunk beneath the surface, Bacon silently vowed to, somehow, find a way to make the sheriff and the captain of the *Adam & Eve* pay for his loss.

At the first light of morning, the council asked the sergeant at arms to get word to Berkeley that Bacon had been captured and the rebellion was over.

CHAPTER 13

Berkeley's Opening Address

June 5, 1676, the Virginia House of Burgesses assembled in the chamber at the state house in Jamestown. The members were relieved their governor had returned, and they were anxious to hear Berkeley's address. They were concerned about the Indians, the taxes, and the fate of Bacon, who had been in jail for the last few days and presently sitting in the back of chambers, next to the sheriff, awaiting Berkeley's arrival.

The governor entered through the back door to no fanfare, flanked by two guards. He climbed up the two steps leading to the lectern, cleared his throat, and unfolded a piece of paper, flattening it on the lectern. The room was silent.

"My constituents, I have many topics to cover on this day, but the most important is the northern aggression on the Indians. I call the northern Burgesses out on their colonists' attacks on the Indians, and demand that they cease at once. Unless I have given direct orders to attack Indians, there will be no further bloodshed for, with, or over Indians. All unordered attacks are henceforth illegal." He looked at the faces of the House. "I hope I make myself clear. The members of the House will be held in strict accountability for not controlling their own people."

Some men grumbled. Some shouted, "Hear, hear."

After the ruckus died down, Berkeley continued. "I also wish to warn you about revolt within our colony. Mr. Richard Lawrence and Mr. William Drummond are rumored to be planning a rebellion against me and members of the council. Their actions will not be tolerated, and I have issued a warrant for their arrest. Be warned of these men and their treasonous acts and keep your distance."

Bacon wondered if Lawrence and Drummond were yet warned of the warrant. He would have to get word to them as soon as he was able. He glanced around the room, but no one looked back at him.

"But if there be joy in the presence of the angels over one sinner that repents, there is joy now, for we have a penitent sinner come before us." Berkeley waved his hand toward Bacon. "Mr. Bacon, the floor is yours." Berkeley took a step backward and sat down in an ornately carved chair.

Bacon rose and walked to the center of the room. He dropped to his knees and said, "I have been guilty of rebellious practices contrary to my duty to his most sacred governor of this county, by the raising of men in arms and marching with them. I have only sought to keep our colony safe from the Indians and have never marched or planned rebellion against any member of the council or against the governor. I beg pardon of the governor, the king, and of God."

Berkeley enjoyed the sight of Bacon on his knees and left him there for an uncomfortable length of time, allowing the room to sit in silence. Finally, Berkeley rose and said, "Mr. Bacon, we appreciate your honesty and humility. I forgive you and God forgives you."

A council member rose. "And all that were with him?"

Berkeley nodded. "And all that were with him. I trust no further incidences will occur in Jamestown or anywhere else on Virginia soil. Mr. Bacon, your bond will be two thousand silver and we demand your promise to keep the peace. As for the future, you have shown yourself to be a strong leader, so if you will live civilly and obediently for a fortnight after this meeting has ended, I will grant you a commission to legally raise and lead forces against the Indians."

"Thank you, Governor. That is all I ever asked."

Berkeley smiled. "Since you have such a loyal following in the colony of Virginia, I will also restore you to your former seat on this council."

"Thank you, Governor." Bacon rose and took his seat among the men in attendance.

Some eyed him with distrust. Some patted him on the shoulder and welcomed him back.

"Finally," Berkeley continued, "I would like to introduce my new war bill. I am proposing we raise taxes to be collected by the sheriffs to pay for this new militia."

After the discussion was finished and all the House members had left the building, Berkeley called for the sheriff. He wrote out a warrant for Bacon's arrest on charges of treason. "I also want messengers sent out by horse and ship to notify militia colonels to come to Jamestown and protect the capital. I've received word that Bacon is working with Lawrence and Drummond in commencing a rebellion against me and the council. The state house needs to be protected from the uprising that is sure to follow Bacon's execution."

The sheriff nodded without questioning Berkeley's change of heart.

The next morning, Berkeley's men broke into Lawrence's home to arrest him, but

Lawrence had been forewarned by Bacon and had fled. They next invaded Drummond's house and found him gone also. They headed for Bacon's, but he was also nowhere to be found.

Berkeley, realizing his act would cause a renewed uprising by Bacon's followers, knew he needed to leave Virginia before he was killed by Bacon or one of his men.

He went to John's house to gather Frances. They would board the next ship bound for London.

"Surely the king will help us," Berkeley told John and Mary.

"Of course he will," Mary said.

"I will simply tell him that Bacon has had too many people declare for him. Frances and I will never be safe as long as Bacon is alive and as long as I am governor. I'll beg the king to send a more rigorous governor in my stead."

"Hopefully, he'll do that," John said.

"Shall we take our silver plate?" Frances asked.

"For what?" Berkeley said.

Frances raised her eyebrows at her husband. "As a gift for the king. One can't merely request an audience with the king and not bring a gift."

"You're correct, my dear. I didn't even think of it," Berkeley said.

"What will you tell the king is the reason for the uprising?" John asked.

"I'll tell him Bacon has no grounds against any one person but against the assembly as a whole. I'll tell him that being the head of said assembly, I seem to be Bacon's greatest grievance."

The fire crackled in the fireplace as the room fell silent. John was happy he wasn't the one who had to sail to London, but he was concerned for his friend. It was a long journey, and Will Berkeley wasn't exactly a young, healthy man. And what would the colony do without a governor while Berkeley was gone? John looked across the room at his friend. Berkeley had grown so old in the last few years. The Indian situation had eaten away at his youth. Bacon had taken the rest. Berkeley looked pale, his deep wrinkles accentuated by the glow of the fire. John couldn't help but feel sorry for him.

"Will, why don't you let Frances go alone? She can certainly gain an audience with the king, and she can probably accomplish more than you can. She could win the king's heart. I hate to say it, but you, my friend, look too weary to even make the journey down to the docks."

"Nonsense. I can make the journey to London just fine." He looked into the fireplace for a while. After a quiet moment, he spoke. "Frances, if for some reason I can't go with you, would you be willing to do as your uncle says and gain an audience with the king in my stead?"

"Of course." Frances also looked into the fireplace, never once at her husband.

CHAPTER 14

Bacon's Invasion

Two weeks later, as Berkeley and Frances were boarding the *Rebecca*, a messenger arrived and told them Bacon was marching east on Jamestown with five hundred men. Berkeley hurried Frances below deck and remained with her, awaiting further word.

"Are you all right, my dear?" Berkeley asked his wife.

"Yes, I'm fine, but I wish we would sail already."

Berkeley asked the captain when they would depart, but the captain said they had trouble with provisions and it might be another day or so. Berkeley was livid.

"I'm sorry, Governor, but we can't sail without the proper provisions. The whole ship would perish in the middle of the ocean."

Within a few hours, Berkeley received a second dispatch stating Bacon was thirty miles upriver with four hundred men.

"How can he be to the west with five hundred men and to the north with four hundred men? Something is wrong here. Find me some reliable news," Berkeley barked at the messenger.

The messenger returned with word that Bacon was ten miles west of town with six hundred men. The news wives were at it again.

"It sounds like we should leave as soon as possible," Frances said.

"I've already checked with the captain. They're not ready to sail yet." Berkeley turned to his messenger. "Tell the militia to pull the cannons from the Brick Fort and move them to Jamestown in preparation for Bacon's attack."

The man nodded.

"And send out scouts to find out exactly where this rebel is. I want a truthful report immediately."

"Yes, sir," the man replied and left the ship.

Berkeley waited for two days, but his scouts never returned. He reluctantly left the safety of the *Rebecca* and rode out to Jamestown to see about the cannons. As he and two of his men walked through the town square on their way to the state house, they heard a cry. "Arms!

Arms! Bacon is within two miles of town!" Berkeley stood on the steps of the state house, saddened and angered that his men had not obeyed his orders. The cannons were lying on wagons, not mounted. No palisades constructed. No garrisons stationed before him. The town looked just as it did when he boarded the *Rebecca* days earlier. He ordered his men to withdraw into the state house and await Bacon and his army.

At two p.m. in the afternoon, Bacon entered Jamestown with men now numbering six hundred and one hundred twenty horses. They surrounded the state house and waited.

An hour later, Berkeley emerged from the front door of the state house, wearing only a white shirt and trousers and wiping sweat from his brow with a cloth. The afternoon summer sun heated the inside of the state house to the temperature of an oven. Berkeley squinted across the square full of men and horses and walked directly toward Bacon. All guns were on Berkeley, but he didn't seem to notice. Bacon held up his hand for his troops to lower their weapons. He then climbed down from his horse and took a step toward Berkeley. The two men met in the middle of the barren yard. There wasn't a sound. Even the birds had silenced.

"I have had quite enough of you and your lawless shenanigans. If you desire my position as governor so badly" — Berkeley ripped open his shirt and exposed his chest—"then I demand you shoot me right now and be done with it."

Bacon shook his head. "I will not shoot you, William Berkeley."

"Then a duel! Challenge me to a duel, sword to sword."

"No, not a duel, either. I have come for one thing and one thing only—a commission to save our colony from the Indians. A commission you have so often promised. We will have it before we go."

Berkeley sighed and walked back toward the state house. The members of his council who were lingering in the doorway and on the front steps watched him pass and enter the building. Bacon looked around at his men and indicated with a nod for some of them to follow him in.

Berkeley sat down at the end of a long table. Perspiration dripped from his forehead and his hands were trembling. A few of his men stood behind him, but didn't make a move to interrupt the meeting that was about to occur.

Bacon sat at the opposite end of the table, leaned back, and crossed his legs. His men stood behind him also, but he waved them away and they stepped backward to the walls.

The two men stared at each other.

Berkeley finally spoke. "I will grant you the commission, but your pay will need to be raised by taxes. I will not pay you myself."

"No. No taxes."

"Then you will not receive the commission. There's no other way to pay for you or the men. If you don't agree to it my way, then you shall have no commission."

Bacon glanced at one of his men. The man nodded to the others, and instantly Bacon's troops inside and outside aimed their muskets at bodyguards, members of Berkeley's assembly, and Berkeley himself. "We will end this, then. We will bring down the state house and all of you in it. We will have your blood," Bacon said.

The troops cocked their muskets.

Berkeley gasped, gawking at Bacon, who almost had a smirk on his face.

No one moved.

"All right, all right! You shall have it! You shall have whatever you want!" yelled Berkeley, throwing his hands up into the air. "Whatever you choose is yours. I will sign a military commission for you in whatever terms you want."

"I want a volunteer army. I don't want to use your war bill and tax the people even more. I want a commission you promised me, so I can tell men to come fight with me—voluntarily."

"Fine." Berkeley began writing down the terms, the sound of the quill pen scratching wildly on the wooden table.

"I also want you to pen a letter to the king saying I am innocent of any wrongdoing and have been acting on authority of you and the council."

Berkeley sighed. "Fine."

"I want every member of the assembly to sign it."

Berkeley looked around the room. "Most of them are not present."

"Then have everyone present sign it and send it to England with your wife. She's on a ship preparing to sail, correct?"

Berkeley ignored the question. "Very well. Is there anything else?"

"Yes, one more thing. I want the captain of the *Adam & Eve* and the sheriff of James City County to reimburse me for the loss of my ship and to be imprisoned for interfering with a Burgess's right to travel unmolested while representing the people in the legislature."

"Very well."

A few days later, the House of Burgesses declared war against the Indians and officially named Nathaniel Bacon its general.

For a few weeks Bacon marched on the Indians with great success, but Burgesses from other counties petitioned Berkeley for relief of their citizens having to join Bacon's militia. They were certain Berkeley would have never granted such a commission to Bacon.

Realizing he had a large amount of community support, Berkeley replied to all of the correspondences, stating he had only given such authority to Bacon while he was held captive and had signed the agreement under duress. He then called up the militias of Middlesex and Gloucester, twelve hundred men strong, to find Bacon and suppress him.

Berkeley sent Frances on ahead to London and joined his men in pursuit of Bacon. While riding with four hundred men through a large field in the hot summer sun, Berkeley fainted while on his horse. He woke up in the field surrounded by a few officers and no militia.

"Where is everyone?"

"They fled. Bacon is closing in on us. We need to get you out of here, Governor."

"We were chasing him, not the other way around."

"Things seemed to have changed, Governor."

Berkeley and the four men with him fled to Accomac, to John's house.

CHAPTER 15

Accomac, Virginia

Mary served John and Berkeley breakfast. The men sat silently and neither touched the food on his plate. John's brow was creased with worry. Berkeley sat with his shoulders hunched.

"He's burnt the whole city to the ground, John. What are we supposed to do now?" Berkeley said as he tapped his chin and stared off into space. His eyes began to fill with tears.

John shook his head. He had warned Berkeley for years that his policies were upsetting the people. He knew years ago that a revolt was in the air. Everyone knew. Everyone saw it coming. Everyone except for Governor Berkeley. What was John supposed to say now? I told you so?

"Thank the good Lord that Frances is not here to witness this devastation," Berkeley continued. "She will be so upset with me if anything has happened to Green Spring. She loves that house." He dropped his head into his hands. "I've made such a mess of things."

"I think Frances may be the answer to all of this chaos. She'll get help from the king and Bacon will be held on charges of treason. We'll see his head soon in a noose and this will all be over."

"Will it really be over then, or will someone else pick up the rebellion where Bacon leaves off?"

John inhaled deeply. "I don't know the answer to that, but I do know Bacon needs to be captured and held accountable."

"And who's going to do that? I've tried unsuccessfully to capture him numerous times, but now he has amassed such an army that we can't get anywhere near him."

"Maybe the king will send soldiers back with Frances."

"I certainly hope so. That's the only way we'll ever stop him."

"Would you gentlemen care for more eggs?" Mary asked, holding a frying pan.

"No, thank you, my dear," John replied.

Berkeley looked down at his plate and shook his head. He hadn't touched the eggs she had already served him.

"Will, why don't you stay here at the house and I'll go into town and see what kind of damage Bacon has done."

"My men said he burnt the whole town, even the state house."

"Well, maybe it's not that bad. Maybe your men are exaggerating."

Berkeley sighed. "If he's touched Green Spring, Frances will hunt him down herself. We won't need the king's army."

A knock came at the door and Mary answered it. The men looked across the small room toward the door and saw one of Berkeley's messengers standing outside. After a moment, Mary returned to the table with a message for Berkeley. He unfolded it and huffed as he read.

"What does it say?" John asked.

"It says Bacon has issued a declaration stating that I have been corrupt as the colony's governor, and has offered a reward to anyone who captures me and takes me to him."

"Surely this is a joke. What would he want with you in his custody?"

"I think he wants to force me to resign. I'm certain he wants my position as governor, at which point he'll probably demand my head." Berkeley laughed a nervous laugh. "Imagine him as governor. The colony wouldn't actually accept him as their governor, would they?" Berkeley's face saddened. He rubbed his temples. "All the work we've done to grow this colony, and that man could destroy it all."

"We'll stop him. Somehow we'll stop him. And don't worry. They'll never capture you here. They don't even know where you are, and even if they did, they don't have boats to sail across the Chesapeake to come get you."

CHAPTER 16

King Charles II

Within days of her arrival in London, Frances gained an audience with the Privy Council, and after explaining to them the deadly upheaval occurring in Virginia, she received permission to speak with the king directly. When she entered the throne room, she was escorted past courtiers and politicians who were waiting in the outer chambers. She felt all eyes upon her. She didn't know if it was because she was a woman going in to see the king or because of her attire. She had always felt like a queen in the colonies, but looking around at the beautiful women of London in their finery, she suddenly felt like a sow in a burlap dress. The styles and fabrics of England had changed while she lived in Virginia the last twenty-seven years. Apparently, the colony didn't keep pace with the latest fashions. She squared her shoulders, held her head high, and attempted to ignore the stares.

She struggled with the heavy box in her arms, a gift for the king. A bead of sweat appeared on her forehead and dripped down her cheek. She ignored it and kept her eyes straight ahead. When the massive double doors opened, she saw the king sitting on his throne at the far end of the room. She took a deep breath and walked forward.

"Lady Berkeley," the sergeant at arms announced.

She stopped in the middle of the room and placed the gift of silver plate on the floor before her. She bowed deeply, discreetly wiping the sweat from her face as she did so.

The king nodded at the sergeant at arms to bring him the gift. After looking over the dented and battered silver plate, the king looked up at Frances.

"How can I help you, Lady Berkeley?"

"Your Highness, I have come at the express desire of my husband, Governor William Berkeley, to beg Your Majesty for help in the colony of Virginia. There has been an evil uprising led by a man named Nathaniel Bacon. He has amassed quite a following and has illegally declared himself the leader of the Virginia militia. The situation has become so desperate that my husband is now in hiding and

I am here pleading for your assistance."

King Charles fondled his goatee. He waved at his servant to bring him a goblet. After he took a drink, he nodded. "Yes, I've heard there have been troubles in Virginia, but I admit I don't have the time or the desire to supervise a distant colony, especially a disorderly one. Your husband can't handle it?"

"No, Your Majesty. Bacon is turning the tide in his favor."

"Has your husband tried to negotiate with him?"

"Yes, Your Majesty, but it has been for naught."

"What does this Bacon want?"

"We believe he wants to take over the colony and become the governor."

The king huffed and held the goblet off to the side for the servant to take. "That will never happen. Governors are appointed by the Lords Proprietors, not by the people's choosing. Have you spoken with Lord Culpepper? He's the proprietor of that land."

"We have tried to but I'm afraid he is not responding to our requests. This is the reason I've come directly to you."

"If what you say it true, Lady Berkeley, then this Bacon has committed treason."

"Yes, Your Majesty."

"How many colonists are following him?"

"I don't know the exact number, but it's

in the hundreds."

The king gestured for the sergeant at arms to come closer.

The man approached the king and fell to his knee.

The king said, "Send a thousand troops to Virginia with Lady Berkeley, and send three commissioners to find out what the hell is going on."

The sergeant at arms rose and backed up a foot before turning around to leave the room.

The king then looked at Frances. "Give them a few days to organize themselves and stow provisions for the journey. They'll squash this rebellion quickly, and your husband will resume his place as governor."

Frances bowed. "I humbly thank Your Majesty."

"Do you have an executioner in Virginia?"

"No, Your Majesty."

"Then I suggest your husband appoint one."

"Yes, Your Majesty."

The king nodded to his soldiers, who opened the double doors behind Frances. She turned and left the throne room. All eyes were again on her as she weaved her way through the crowd, but she didn't concern herself with their judgments. She had received what she had come for. She would soon be back in Virginia—back on her own throne.

Since she had a few days before the ships would sail, she went to Leeds Castle to see her brother and meet her niece. As she hadn't seen the house in twenty seven years, she had completely forgotten how astounding Leeds Castle was. When the carriage pulled out of the woods and the castle appeared in the distance, it took her breath away. It seemed larger than she remembered. Melancholy filled her chest as she recalled those days barricaded inside the castle walls following the war. Her family had patiently waited for an entire year for her uncle John to come save them. When he finally arrived, they were whisked away to his ship, where they endured a two-month journey to Virginia. She didn't realize until this moment that she had blocked out all of those terrible memories. She hadn't thought about this place or any part of her family's struggle in over two decades.

What would it have been like to stay in England? A wave of sadness washed over her. What would it have been like to live here with her family? Her father wouldn't have been killed in Virginia. Her mother wouldn't have died of a broken heart. There was no use in thinking such things. They'd had no choice but to leave. Her father had been a colonel in the king's army, and when the king was beheaded, Virginia became the only safe place for her family. Her father would have been executed if they had stayed in England. Her mother would have died of a broken heart either way. It had been so long ago, Frances seldom thought about them or missed them anymore, but at this moment, she wondered if she would have grown to become the same woman had her parents lived.

Upon arriving at the castle, she was escorted into a grand room where she was instructed to wait for Master Culpepper to welcome her. It all seemed rather formal, and Frances realized she had become a Virginian. She was no longer the proper English girl she was raised to be. Though thoughts of living in England were wistful and dreamy, she knew she didn't belong here anymore, not with her dated attire and lack of pretentiousness.

"Frances?" Alex trotted into the room, dressed in a velvet doublet, matching breeches, and leather boots. His smile was radiant. "What are you doing here?"

Frances smiled as her eyes fell on her handsome and happy brother. "Alex, you look wonderful!"

"As do you, my dear sister." Alex gave her a long hug. "Now, what brings you to London?"

"I came to see the king. We are in dire circumstances in Virginia."

"What's happening? We've received letters from Uncle John as he was looking to reach Lord Culpepper, but there was nothing we could do to help."

"It's all right. The king is taking care of it."

Margaretta entered the room, holding hands with a young girl about seven or eight years old. The child had locks of curly brown hair, and she looked like a cherub with her blue eyes, large and curious.

"Margaretta, this is my dear sister Lady Frances Berkeley. Frances, this is Margaretta and young Catherine."

Frances couldn't take her eyes off the child. Catherine was a Culpepper through and through. Frances fell to her knees and held out her hands toward the girl. "Catherine? I'm your aunt Frances. It is so nice to meet you. Come give me a hug."

Catherine let go of her mother's hand and walked slowly toward Frances. Once she reached her, Frances wrapped her arms around the girl. With a huge smile on her face, Frances rose and greeted Margaretta.

"Lady Culpepper, I am so pleased to finally make your acquaintance."

"And I, yours, Lady Berkeley. I'm sorry I've been unable to help with the problems in Virginia. Lord Culpepper resides in London and it's been years since we've communicated."

"That's all right. I've spoken to the king directly and he's sending an army. Everything will be fine once they arrive."

The three adults and young Catherine visited for a few days until it was time for Frances to board the Virginia-bound ship. It was a tearful good-bye, but Frances would be forever grateful that she finally got to meet her niece, something she never thought would happen. The child was beautiful, and after seeing Alex and Margaretta together, Frances understood why Alex couldn't stay in Virginia. The sight of them made Frances question her own relationships, but she realized one could either have love or status. It would be highly unlikely to have both in this lifetime.

CHAPTER 17

Revolt Over

A knock came on John's door on a cool October day, and he answered it to find one of Berkeley's messengers with beads of sweat on his forehead. The man looked like he had run all the way from Jamestown.

"Sir, I need to speak with Governor Berkeley."

John stepped out of the way and waved his arm for the man to enter. Berkeley rose from the dining table and walked toward them.

"What is the news?" Berkeley asked.

"Nathaniel Bacon is dead, sir."

"What? Who killed him?"

"No one killed him, sir. He died of the bloody flux. The revolt is over, sir."

"It's over?" He turned to John. "Did you hear that John? It's over!"

John cocked his head. "Has anyone seen

the body?"

The man shook his head. "It is believed his soldiers burned it because of contamination."

"Is it safe for me to return home?" Berkeley asked.

"Yes, sir. Everyone has returned to their homes," the messenger said.

"What do you think, John?" Berkeley asked.

"I think, if this is indeed true, you need to return to Jamestown and claim your place before someone else steps forward to lead Bacon's revolt."

CHAPTER 18

1677, Return to Green Spring

Berkeley sent scouts to see whether or not Bacon's death was fact. They checked Jamestown and Green Spring, and indeed, there was no militia wandering around Jamestown and no soldiers near Berkeley's home.

A month later on a chilly fall day, seventy-one-year-old Berkeley, with John by his side, arrived in Jamestown and was sickened by the destruction. Beautiful buildings lay in heaps of ash. There were no longer outlines of streets, as debris covered every inch of the ground. The men were forced to step over piles of rubble as they walked the city. Everything that had made Jamestown a delightful city—bushes, trees, flowers, shops, homes with charming porches, church steeples—was gone.

The state house was nothing more than charred beams, sticking straight up like a deformed tree against the blue, cloudless sky. John, Berkeley, and a handful of bodyguards wandered around the remains, searching for anything to salvage, anything recognizable, but there was nothing left.

Berkeley and John rode out to Green Spring. The trees lining Sugar Row and the mulberry bushes were still standing, and the men were thrilled to find the house wasn't burnt to the ground. They entered the front door, which had been splintered by an axe, and found the home looted. Large pieces of furniture remained, but every drawer was missing, every door opened, and every nook empty. Anything that could not be carried and stolen had been smashed or destroyed. Berkeley exited through the back door and looked across his vast expanse of land. His crops had been pilfered or destroyed. The fields were flat, but thank God the house was still standing.

Berkeley rejoined John in the middle of the parlor, and they were turning in circles, still taking in the destruction when Frances and the three English commissioners sent by the king entered. Frances's jaw hung open and her eyes were large. She didn't acknowledge her husband or her uncle as she viewed the devastation that was once her grand home. The commissioners stood next to her, also agape.

Finally her eyes met her husband's and he shook his head. "Frances, I'm sorry. They've destroyed our home."

"I can see that." She clenched her teeth and placed her hands on her hips. "We will certainly put an end to them, and they will pay for what they've done. I've brought back an army of one thousand to find Bacon and put an end to the revolt."

"The revolt is over. Bacon is dead," John said.

Frances's jaw dropped for the second time. "It's over?"

Berkeley and John nodded.

After a moment, Frances said, "Then we will use our army to round up the remaining revolutionists and see them hanged."

Berkeley had never seen his wife this angry. This would not end well for the men who destroyed her beloved home.

Following the Yuletide season, Berkeley's men built a triangular scaffold in the town square in front of the burned-out state house. It was reminiscent of the one used generations ago at Tyburn. With its three legs, over twenty people could be simultaneously hung, and Berkeley planned on using every space available. His men rounded up twenty-two colonists who were instrumental in the revolt, including the former governor of Albemarle, William Drummond.

Berkeley had a table and chair brought into the middle of the town square, and took his seat in what used to be a road. The cloudy winter sky threatened snow, but the cold weather wouldn't deter Berkeley from the job before him. He pulled his scarf tighter around his neck and waved at his men to bring the accused before him. The twenty-two prisoners were paraded through the black rubble that once was Jamestown and brought before Berkeley. He coldly acknowledged and sentenced each man, never asking a question of any of them, never hearing any testimony, never allowing any sort of fair trial. Following the predetermined sentencing, the prisoners were escorted, hands tied behind their backs, toward the scaffolding.

When William Drummond was brought before him, shuffling his feet with his hands tied and his shoulders hunched, Berkeley said, "Mr. Drummond, I am more glad to see you than any man in Virginia. You shall be hanged within a half hour." Berkeley motioned for his men to take Drummond away. As with other prisoners, that was the extent of Drummond's trial and sentencing.

What seemed like the entire population of Virginia had gathered in the town square. Thousands shivered in the cold and watched the proceedings. Some cheered as each man was led toward the scaffold. Women's sobs were heard each time the cheering died down. The three commissioners, standing next to a proud Frances, watched in horror. They were not appointed to do anything except report back to the king.

When the mock trials ended, each man was led up the steps of the scaffold and his head placed in a rope. Berkeley's men tightened the nooses. The last prisoner to have his head placed in the rope was William Drummond. Berkeley smiled at him when their eyes locked. Drummond's face held no expression. His eyes pulled away from Berkeley as he searched the crowd for his wife. His face softened when he found her, next to a pale John Culpepper. John's son stood behind them, his face red with fury.

Before the men were hanged, a young man unrolled a piece of paper and read, "Traitors and rebels, in the name of the king of England, the governor of Virginia, and the people of Jamestown, you are to be hanged until dead. Let this be a lesson to all here that treason is not and will never be tolerated in the colony of Virginia."

The man then read each of the names aloud. "John Baptista, Giles Bland, William Cookson, James Crews, William Davis, William Drummond..." The names continued until all twenty-two had been read. At the conclusion, the young man nodded to the executioners, and the condemned suddenly found their feet dangling beneath them.

Some of those in attendance yelled and applauded. Most did not.

Following the hangings, Berkeley seized all of the dead men's property, leaving their wives and families homeless, including the now widowed Sarah Drummond. Berkeley said it served her right for spreading propaganda about him. The other news wives were held up to public scrutiny over the next few weeks and months. Mrs. Grindon was the first woman in the history of the colony to be placed in the stocks. Mrs. Cheezeman was taunted and humiliated following the execution of her husband. Mrs. Lloyd was so abused by Berkeley's men, she went into premature labor and died during the birth. Mrs. Drummond left town, a broken woman with nothing left.

As spring of the following year descended onto the colony in a warm blanket of sunshine and peaceful days, men slowly began to rebuild Jamestown. Rubble was removed and new buildings rose in its place. Frances didn't venture into town. She remained at Green Spring, restoring her home to its original glory, having fences and furniture rebuilt and gardens and fields replanted.

On a spring afternoon, she held a dinner party for the king's three commissioners, who were preparing to set sail back to England the following morning. She invited all the members of the council, even the ones she suspected of plotting against her husband. The event was glorious, with pheasant and wild boar, and brandy and wine flowing like water.

As the party was coming to an end, two members of the council bid their good-byes and were prepared to walk the three miles back to Jamestown. But Frances, still harboring suspicions about their loyalty to her husband, wasn't done yet.

"No, no, gentlemen. I would hate for you to walk all that way. I've arranged a ride for you." She escorted the men to the front of the house and pulled both doors open at the same time in a grand gesture. What sat before them left both men speechless. She had hired an undertaker's wagon to take the men to town.

"Is this some sort of joke, madam?" one of the men said.

"No, it's no joke. I've arranged a comfortable ride for you." Frances smiled.

"My dear lady, your sense of humor is lost on me. We will walk," a second man said.

As the men exited the house in a huff, John approached his niece. "That was an evil thing to do, Frances."

"And what they did to my husband and my home wasn't evil? They deserve it...and more."

John shook his head.

Frances threw her head back and laughed, certain the men walking down Sugar Row could hear her, which made the joke all the better.

* * *

When the commissioners returned to England and reported the events to the king, he had only one comment. "That old fool has put to death more people in that country than I did here for the murder of my father. Send word to Berkeley that he needs to come to England and answer for his actions."

CHAPTER 19

Albemarle, Carolina

"They hung William Drummond in front of my very eyes," Johnny said, shaking his head and looking down at the dusty road as he walked.

George Durant sighed and looked across the field as he chewed on a long piece of grass. "How could they do that to him? He was a governor, one appointed by Berkeley himself. Surely he deserved more respect than Berkeley showed him."

"He certainly did. I'll tell you, Berkeley has been a friend of my father's for years and years, but honestly, I think the old man has lost his mind. He flip-flopped between denying a militia commission to Bacon, then granting it to him, and then adamantly denying he ever did so. I know my father has been by Berkeley's side as his advisor for decades, and I'm certain my father advised him against all of this nonsense."

"Maybe your father is crazy, too!" Durant grinned.

"George, if you weren't my friend, I would put a shot right between your eyes for saying that. My father is and has always been an upstanding man. He's intelligent and fair. He studied law in his youth, so he not only understands the difficulties of the common settler, he also knows the legalities of the colony. I know he's fought against Berkeley's ridiculous taxes. I'm sure he warned Berkeley against hanging all those men, too."

"I don't know about the hangings, but the taxes are only getting worse. Since Thomas Miller arrived in Albemarle, it seems like the taxation has been increasing every day."

"Who is this Miller, and why doesn't the governor the Lords Proprietors appointed get here already?"

"They appointed a man named Eastchurch. From what I understand, Eastchurch and Miller were traveling together from London. They stopped in Nevis for supplies, and Eastchurch met a rich woman there and married her. So, he has been detained for an undetermined time, and apparently, he sent Miller on ahead to act as a surrogate governor and gave him full commission with great latitude to run Albemarle. I haven't seen proof of any such commission, though."

"Do you think Miller is corrupt?"

Durant nodded. "Undoubtedly. Before he arrived here, he first sailed to Virginia and hired about thirty of Bacon's supporters to act as his bodyguards. If he wasn't corrupt, he wouldn't need the protection."

"Why would Bacon's men side now with a corrupt government when they've been fighting against it for so long?"

"I guess money speaks louder than loyalty to many men in this county, and besides, they had nowhere else to go. Berkeley was going to run them out of Virginia or eventually hang them, whichever struck his fancy at the moment."

Johnny huffed. "I told you Berkeley is crazy."

Durant looked down the road and groaned.

"What?" asked Johnny.

"I'm just wondering if we should put together a group of men and give Miller a proper welcome. I know everyone is tired of the taxes, and maybe we can swing Bacon's supporters to our cause. If they're here in Albemarle, we might as well use them."

Johnny grinned. "Are you talking about running Miller out of town?"

Durant narrowed his eyes. "I'm talking about reclaiming our government by whatever means necessary."

"That's treason, George. We'll end up hung just like Drummond."

"That's freedom, Johnny. Berkeley doesn't run things around here. Apparently nobody does. If Eastchurch stays in Nevis and never shows up, we'll never have to answer for it."

A few weeks later, the rebels heard that Eastchurch had indeed arrived in the colonies, but in Virginia, not Carolina. The rebels sent word to him that he wasn't welcome in Albemarle and should stay away — or else.

CHAPTER 20

Berkeley Summoned

A messenger from the king arrived the spring of 1677 and delivered a royal summons to Berkeley. His hand shook as he read it at the breakfast table. "Do you think we did the right thing, dear?" he asked Frances.

"Of course we did. You couldn't allow those lawbreakers to run amok without a consequence for their actions. They committed treason, and the king is the one who told me you should appoint an executioner. Why would he want you to do so and then not use the man?"

"Then why is the king summoning me?"

"Perhaps he wants to congratulate you on doing such a fine job." Frances sipped warm cider from a newly delivered china cup.

Berkeley shook his head. "It says here he wants me to come to London and *answer* for my actions. Doesn't sound like congratulations to me."

"Don't worry, husband. Once King Charles hears your side of the story, he'll be very pleased you were the strong governor you are. Anyone else would have folded under the pressure. Look at Eastchurch. He showed up in Jamestown and simply dropped dead because the stress was too much for him to take. Who's going to rule Albemarle now?"

"I'm certain I don't know, but I'm happy we didn't have to put together an army to protect the man. We have enough troubles here in Jamestown. We don't need to fight Albemarle's battles, too. I guess the Lords Proprietors will send over someone new eventually, or maybe the residents will kill each other and the problem will solve itself."

"Well, head down to the dock and find a ship for your passage and I'll pack for you. You can see your brother while you're in London. It's been, what, thirty years since you've seen him? That will be a nice visit for you. And if you have time, you can stop by Leeds Castle and check on Alex, too. I hope he and Margaretta are doing well. Wait until you see little Catherine. She'll steal your heart with those blue eyes."

Berkeley rose and kissed his wife on the forehead. "I'll be happy to check on Alex for you, my dear. I guess I'd better get going if I'm going to find a ship. We don't want to keep the king waiting."

Berkeley left Virginia within the week, but he became dreadfully ill on the voyage. Once he arrived in London, he went straight to his brother's home. It wasn't much of a reunion, as he didn't rise from his sickbed for two weeks. He was racked with fever and pain, and the doctors had no idea what was ailing him. They tried many remedies, but none were of any use.

The sergeant at arms from the king's court visited to tell Berkeley he had been granted an audience with the king, but when the sergeant entered the room, he found Berkeley unconscious. Upon hearing that Berkeley had been that way for two weeks, the sergeant at arms left without delivering the message.

CHAPTER 21

Kidnap

As fall deposited a blanket of brown and yellow leaves on the ground in Albemarle, Johnny, Durant, and Bird gathered as many men as they could find, including some of Bacon's old supporters whom Johnny knew from meetings in Virginia. The group armed itself and in the middle of the night descended upon the homes of the unsuspecting members of Miller's cabinet. One by one, the men arrested and kidnapped Timothy Biggs, John Nixon, Henry Hudson, and others. They confiscated every document and record they could find, and moved the prisoners to Durant's barn.

Johnny entered the back door of the governor's house in the middle of the town square. He tiptoed up the staircase in the dim moonlight coming in from the window at the top of the stairs. Since he had been in this house many times, he knew which bed chamber would belong to Miller. He paused outside of the door and listened to the man snore.

When he entered the room, he walked straight to the bed and poked his pistol into Miller's ribs.

Only the light of the moon illuminated the room, but it was enough for Miller to see Johnny's face before him.

"What is going on here, Culpepper?"

"Slowly get out of bed and get dressed. You're coming with me."

"Coming where? Why are you holding a gun to my head?"

"Rise from your bed and you will not be harmed."

Nervously, Miller did as he was told. He rose, stepped into his trousers, and put his shoes on. Johnny bound his hands behind his back and escorted him down the stairs. When they emerged from the house, Durant and Bird approached them.

"Put him in the wagon. We'll put him with the others," Bird said.

Johnny led Miller to the wagon and helped him up.

"I don't know what you men are up to, but you'll pay for this," Miller threatened.

Durant stuck a pistol under his chin. "Your threats are over, Miller."

Miller didn't say another word as they

rode to Durant's house. Johnny kept a pistol on him for the entire ride.

When they arrived, Johnny climbed down from the wagon and pulled the rope, causing Miller to fall from the wagon and land on the ground with a thud. Johnny reached down, took Miller's arm, and helped him up. They entered Durant's barn, where all the members of Miller's cabinet had already been placed, tied to each post and beam like animals. After tying Miller to a post, Johnny walked to the house to talk to Durant and Bird.

"We can't hold Miller for no reason. We need to officially charge him with something and place him on trial," said Durant.

"He certainly deserves to be locked up forever, but what are you thinking to charge him with?" Johnny asked.

"Everyone knows he's a heavy drinker with a bad habit of spewing irreverence toward the church and disloyalty to the king. I think that would be a good start," Durant said.

Johnny, Durant, and Bird acted as their own government and charged Miller with blasphemy and treason. They placed him in irons until they could find a way to hold a trial. With all the cabinet members tied up in the barn, there was no more court system.

The trio spent months going through the confiscated accounts and registers. They found a lot of irregularities in the records of the colony's tax monies. Johnny drew up a remonstrance, explaining to the Albemarle residence why Miller had been imprisoned and urging the colonists to stand with them against Miller and his cabinet. He posted it on the door of the governor's house. It stated Miller had denied free elections, had cheated the county out of a hundred thirty thousand pounds of tobacco, and had illegally raised the tax by two hundred fifty pounds per person.

The response of the colonists was everything Johnny had hoped for. Nearly every citizen backed the rebellion, standing together against the corrupt governor. The mob expressed their anger over the negligent Lord Proprietors and slightly over the king.

CHAPTER 22

Green Spring

In September, Frances received a letter from London. She hadn't heard from her husband since he left Jamestown nearly five months earlier, but she was sure he'd had enough time to arrive in London, visit his brother, and she was confident he was now enjoying family and friends in London as he awaited an audience with the king. The handwriting on the envelope didn't look familiar, and she turned it over and over. She sat down at the dining table, hoping the letter was good news. Surely the king wouldn't reprimand her husband for simply maintaining the status quo of the colony. Her husband had been instrumental in holding the colony together for decades, and he made the crown a very nice income through taxes and tariffs. The king would certainly be pleased with the way Will handled the uprising, even though the king had footed the expense to send all those soldiers over for nothing. Still, the incident was over now and all was well.

She unfolded the paper. The bottom was signed by Will's brother. Frances felt a flame of fear rise up her spine.

My dearest sister Frances,

It is to my great regret that I write to inform you of the passing of my brother in July. He arrived on my doorstep looking a fright, and he did not leave his sickbed even once since his arrival. One of the king's guards came to see him the day before he died. I believe he was here to grant Will an audience with the king. but once the envoy saw him, he did not deliver the message. It would have been useless, as Will died the following morning. We have buried him here in the family plot. I assume it is your responsibility to deliver the news to his constituents, and you should ask someone to inform the king or the Lords Proprietors of the vacancy in the governorship. I did not want to step into your business and get in your way, as I did not know what arrangements Will had made prior. Please know how sorry I am that this happened, but I was very happy to see my brother, as it had been many years. Our reunion was a brief but joyous one.

Again, I am so very sorry.
Your brother,
Sir John Berkeley

Frances stared blankly at the piece of paper in her hands and read it over and over again. At the age of forty-three, she was now twice widowed. She felt tears come to her eyes and wished they were tears of sorrow, tears of a widow grieving a lost love, but she knew they were only tears of frustration for being put in this situation yet again. She squared her shoulders and wiped her eyes. This was no time to fall apart. She needed to maintain control of the colony, especially without her husband.

She walked to the desk in the corner of the room and sat down. She grabbed a sheet of paper and penned a message to the only person she could think of to help her through this tragedy. She sent for her uncle John.

When John arrived, he found his usually effervescent niece lying in bed, a damp cloth covering her forehead, and the curtains drawn. He dismissed the servant girl who sat at the side of the bed. Once the door closed, he sat in the empty chair next to Frances. "My dear, what has happened? I only got word you needed me here and that it was an emergency."

Frances opened her eyes. "Will is dead."

"What?"

"He died at his brother's house in London." She pulled the letter out from under her pillow and handed it to John.

She sobbed as he struggled to read the letter in the dim light. When he finished, he looked at Frances. "Oh, this is terrible news."

"I know. What am I to do, Uncle?" She dabbed her eyes with a lace-trimmed handkerchief.

John sighed. "I'm not sure, my dear. I guess the House needs to be informed. Do you know anything about appointing a new governor or what we should do?"

"I'm not concerned with politics right now. I've lost my husband."

"I know. I'm sorry. We'll deal with the colonial business later."

Frances sat up in bed as if the last five minutes had never happened. "Speaking of colonies, I just heard that something dreadful has happened in Albemarle."

John felt the flames of adrenaline rise up the back of his neck. He raised his eyebrows and waited for her to continue.

"I heard the acting governor and his entire council have been kidnapped by rebels."

"That's terrible news. Who's responsible?"

Frances shrugged. "I heard Johnny is involved.

CHAPTER 23

Election

Since all the members of the Albemarle legislature were being held prisoner, Johnny and his friends needed to find a way to keep the colony organized. The first step was to elect a new cabinet. Thirty members of the community met in Durant's home and held court in his parlor.

"We still need to collect a moderate tax to keep the town running smoothly. Is there a nomination for the tax collector?" Durant asked the group.

Bird raised his hand. "I nominate the most honest person we know — Johnny Culpepper."

The role of tax collector had traditionally been one that no one liked, and Johnny knew it would often be unpleasant to collect monies from friends, but Johnny was pleased that his associates considered him honest enough to do the job.

"I second the nomination," a voice rose from the back of the room.

"All in favor, say aye," Durant said.

The group of men said aye.

"Opposed?" Durant said.

No one spoke.

"Congratulations, Johnny, you are Albemarle's new tax collector," Durant said.

Johnny nodded. He didn't want to be a key member of the new government and wasn't pleased to have to go door to door demanding money, but he'd known overthrowing the local government would cause a void that needed to be filled. He would collect the taxes and place them in safekeeping, and soon he would find someone else to take the position. He didn't want to end up being hated by his friends simply because of a job title.

"Are we going to vote on a new governor?" Johnny asked.

Durant hesitated as the din in the room increased. Finally he raised his voice. "Please keep it quiet, gentlemen. I know we're weary of being told what to do by a single person in power. I think we should run the colony as a group. I was thinking you, Mr. Bird, and I could hold the office as a mere formality."

"I don't want anything to do with running the colony. I'm sorry," Bird said.

Durant looked at Johnny. "Well, then, it looks like it's just you and me, Johnny."

One of the things everyone hated about Miller was the fact he simultaneously held the offices of council member, acting governor, customs collector, and judge. Johnny wasn't thrilled about recreating the same scenario, but Durant was his friend. They were in this together, and Johnny knew they shouldn't appear divided in front of the other residents. He nodded.

"Is everyone in agreement?"

The room again said aye.

"Good, it's settled, then. Now, the next item on our agenda is the fate of Miller and his cabinet. Does anyone have an idea of what we should do with them?"

A man in the back stood up. "We should hang them in the market square!"

"No, no," Durant said. "If the king has a problem with what we've done, I don't want to be charged with murder. We currently have no court to try them in, so we certainly don't want them executed...not without a trial anyway."

"Then leave them locked up," someone else chimed in.

"But they're in *my* barn," Durant said, half joking, half serious.

"Why don't we build a new place to house them, a jail of sorts?"

"Now, that's an idea I like," Durant said.

"I'd like everyone to explore where this jail can be built, and we'll use the first of the tax monies Johnny collects to pay for it."

The crowd mumbled and nodded.

"I guess our meeting is finished. We will reconvene in one month's time."

The men rose and chatted as they left Durant's house. Everyone seemed pleased with the outcome of the meeting.

Once they were all gone, Durant said to Johnny, "See? That's how a town meeting should be run. Every man has a voice. Even if we disagree, we can still come to some kind of consensus."

Johnny nodded.

"Why are you so quiet?"

"I'm not thrilled with being known as the customs collector. People hate him."

"Don't be silly. No one here hates you, Johnny. You are one of the most beloved citizens in Albemarle."

"For now," Johnny mumbled as he grabbed his hat off the table and headed toward the door.

CHAPTER 24

Albemarle

Even though Frances was in the depths of grief, John left her and set out for Albemarle. He needed to find out the extent of his son's involvement with the uprising. He rode all through the night, with low-hanging branches nearly taking his head off at least half a dozen times. If his son was in trouble, John needed to be there. Everything else would have to wait, including his inconsolable niece and the vacancy left in the Virginia governor's office.

John arrived at the market square of Albemarle early in the morning and didn't know where else to begin his search for his son but the governor's house. Nailed to the door was the bill urging citizens to stand against the tyranny of Miller and his cabinet. It was signed at the bottom by Johnny. Frances had been right. Johnny was involved — up to his neck, it seemed.

John rapped sharply on the door and a slave girl answered.

"Is Johnny Culpepper here?" he asked.

"Yes, sir, he's having breakfast on the back porch."

John stepped off the porch and ran around the house, leaving the slave girl standing in the open doorway. His legs were stiff from riding for so long and were cramping by the time he reached the back porch. He found his son enjoying the morning sun while reading a book. "Johnny! What is going on?"

"Father, what are you doing here?"

"I heard there was some sort of mutiny or rebellion."

Johnny chuckled. "Not much of a rebellion. Nothing like you experienced in Jamestown. But yes, I guess mutiny is a pretty good description."

John sat down in the nearest chair, exhausted from no sleep. He massaged his aching calves. "What is going on? What happened?"

"We arrested Miller and the members of his cabinet. They were running the colony illegally, so we put an end to it."

"Arrested? I heard kidnapped."

"I guess it depends on who you ask." Johnny laughed. "Father, do you want some breakfast?"

"No, I want to know what's going on.

Where is Miller now?"

"In George Durant's barn."

"And the others?"

"Same place."

"How long are you going to keep them there?"

"Until the Lords Proprietors tell us what to do with them."

"So, you've notified the Lords Proprietors of the events?"

Johnny grinned. "No, not yet, but we will."

"When?" John was in no mood for his son's antics.

"When we're ready." Johnny set his book on the table. "Are you sure I can't get you some breakfast?"

John realized butting heads with his stubborn son would get him nowhere. He softened his tone. "I guess I do need to eat something, and then you can tell me from the beginning what's happening here."

CHAPTER 25

1678, Miller Escapes

The Lords Proprietors received word of the scandal in Albemarle, and though they weren't overly concerned about the small colony, they knew they needed to do something about Miller, who still sat in jail, albeit the new one in the center of town instead of the barn behind Durant's house. They allowed the acting council to bring Miller to trial.

The council ordered Miller to be transported from the jail to the governor's house in the custody of the county marshal. After all this time, he would finally stand trial for blasphemy and treason. The marshal unlocked the door to the jail cell and escorted Miller to the waiting wagon. His hands were not bound, as there was a deputy holding a gun on Miller. Soon, the trio began its thirteen-mile trek while Durant, Bird, and Johnny Culpepper waited for them at the governor's house.

Miller sat quietly in the back of the wagon listening to his escorts talk on the front bench. They were having a disagreement about something, and their conversation grew more heated with each passing mile. The wagon bounced down the road and entered a narrow, tree-lined area. Miller took advantage of the men not watching him, and inched his way closer and closer to the back of the wagon. Just before it entered the town square, where the trees were densest, Miller hopped off the wagon and ran into the forest. He was already hidden well within the woodland when he heard the marshal yell, "Where did he go?" Miller heard the wagon wheels stop grinding and the two men jump down and chase him into the trees.

He stopped behind a gigantic weeping willow, looking around wildly, wondering which way to run. He heard twigs snap as the men in pursuit drew closer. He slid around to the other side of the tree as the men passed him. After a few moments their voices grew fainter, and Miller tiptoed in the other direction, entering deeper into the woods. He would head north. He would find a ship bound for London as soon as he reached water. He would stow away if he had to. He would report to the Lords Proprietors what had happened. Surely they didn't know or they would have sent help by now. He would explain how this group of hoodlums had kidnapped him and his entire cabinet and held them prisoner. He would see Culpepper, Durant, and Bird hanged for this, especially Culpepper for breaking into his house and holding a gun to his head.

After a few days of plodding through the forest and avoiding snakes and Indians, Miller finally reached the water. He promised a ship captain great rewards if the man gave Miller passage to England. The captain, not being from Albemarle, didn't know what had happened in the colony, but Miller's story sounded credible so he agreed to the deal.

Upon Miller's arrival in London, he entered the Lords Proprietors' meeting, dressed in the rags he had escaped in, and reported the recent events in Albemarle. Contrary to what he thought would happen, the Lords Proprietors, having already heard about Miller and his cabinet being placed in jail, didn't seem anxious to seek retribution for Miller's predicament. They didn't have the military means to do anything themselves, and they didn't want to get the king involved. They knew how upset he had been over the revolt in Jamestown, and didn't want to anger him further. It was entirely possible that the king would rid them of their proprietorship and perhaps even take their titles for allowing something so disgraceful to happen. And unbeknownst to Miller, the proprietors had sent someone to find out the details of the uprising. The man had sailed to Albemarle and returned to London without Miller's knowledge. After hearing from their representative that everything was running fine in the colony and that Johnny Culpepper, who was acting as the tax collector, would soon be on his way to London with the tax receipts, they set aside any further concerns about the colony. Today, they politely listened to Miller and took notes about the people involved, and then they dismissed him.

Miller was livid.

The Lords Proprietors were nervous. Now that Miller was in London and might cause a public uproar about the happenings in the colony, the Lords Proprietors sent for Culpepper, demanding he arrive immediately.

Johnny Culpepper arrived in London three months later. He wasn't greeted warmly, but he wasn't thrown in jail either. An inquest was held, and while Culpepper admitted his rebellious acts, he denied any wrongdoing as far as collecting customs. He had been elected by the people and had done the job as best he could. He wasn't in possession of all the customs receipts, as he had left the colony so quickly at the Lords Proprietors' urgent request, so he paid a five-hundred-pound bond to the proprietors, with the promise that he would return with the missing receipts within the year.

The proprietors were satisfied that the

problem had been resolved.

Miller heard Culpepper had been sent for, so he'd appeared at the meetings daily, hoping to see Culpepper charged with embezzlement, but Miller was always requested to remain outside of the meeting place which was Lord Shaftesbury's residence. He spent three chilly days sitting on a stone bench in front of the stately manor, one of them in the rain. He would remain there as long as it took. At one point, he pounded on the front door with his fists, demanding to come face to face with his kidnapper. The Lords Proprietors refused him entry. Tiring of Miller's complaints and accusations, they told him the running of Albemarle was no longer his concern, and they threatened to have him arrested if he interrupted their meetings again. Miller was sent away. He never saw Culpepper.

CHAPTER 26

December 1679, Treason

After the Lords Proprietors didn't respond to Miller's tale of kidnapping and embezzlement, Miller found his way to the king's court and appealed to the Privy Council. Contrary to the Lords Proprietors, the council showed great interest in the possibility that the king was not receiving his share of the customs. They encouraged Miller to file a formal petition, stating that the rebels illegally seized and controlled Albemarle without any authority, and that they were collecting taxes and keeping them. Embezzling from the king was a treasonous offense. At the formal inquest by the Privy Council, Miller brought forth men to testify against Johnny Culpepper, even though Johnny wasn't there to defend himself. Henry Hudson and John Taylor—friends of Miller—spoke against Culpepper, and three days later, by order of the Privy Council, Johnny Culpepper was charged with treason.

By the time the charges were ordered, Johnny had finished his business with the Lords Proprietors and was about to return to Albemarle. He was waiting for the ship to secure provisions and was speaking with a man on the dock when the king's guards appeared.

"Mr. John Culpepper!" one of the guards bellowed.

Johnny turned around. "Ay, I am John Culpepper."

Two guards approached him and grabbed his arms.

Johnny struggled to free himself from their grasp but to no avail.

"Mr. John Culpepper, by command of King Charles the Second, King of England, Scotland, and Ireland, you are under arrest for embezzlement of the king's funds and are charged with treason against His Royal Majesty."

Johnny tried to pull away from the guards, shaking his head furiously. "No, there must be some mistake. I have just given all the customs receipts I had to the Lords Proprietors. I haven't embezzled anything."

"You can state your case in the royal court."

The men tied his arms behind his back and wrapped the rope around his waist. They mounted their horses and pulled Johnny behind them.

A crowd watched, but no one stepped in to help. One didn't get in the way of the king's guards unless one wanted to be thrown into prison. Johnny looked at the faces of the spectators as he was yanked forward. He almost stumbled but caught his footing. He wanted to tell someone to report this to the Lords Proprietors, but he wasn't sure if it was them who had reported the embezzlement to the king. He didn't recognize a face in the crowd. He didn't know what to do.

Johnny sat in the prison at Newgate for weeks, repeatedly requesting a speedy trial. His request wasn't heeded, and even if it had been, he was probably only hastening his own demise. He had no receipts. He had no proof of his innocence. The more time he spent alone in the jail cell, the more certain he was that Miller was at the bottom of this. If the Lords Proprietors were responsible, they would have held him during their meetings, wouldn't they? How could he fight Miller? And the Privy Council had taken over the investigation. Johnny certainly couldn't battle them, not without proof.

A great sadness fell over him as his monotonous days in jail stretched to weeks. There were moments when he thought he would probably die in prison before ever getting a trial, and who knew if it would be a fair trial? Johnny had no defense. No matter the reasons, he had kidnapped Miller. He had illegally collected taxes. He had no receipts for the monies he had collected. He would probably hang.

After a long month, Johnny was finally moved to London, but instead of being brought before the council for trial, he was placed in a cold, damp cell in the Tower. Here he would wait.

He asked the guard to send word to John Culpepper in Jamestown.

CHAPTER 27

Intervention

When John received word of his son's arrest, he traveled down to Albemarle to find out what had happened. From what he understood, there were no legal issues with the events in Albemarle or with the Lords Proprietors, so what could have transpired to get his son thrown in jail? He rode to Durant's house and found him there with Bird.

"Mr. Durant, I came to see if you know what happened to my son."

Durant shook his head. "According to the Lords Proprietors, Johnny's been arrested for embezzlement."

"Embezzlement? Charged by the Lords Proprietors?" John felt the bile rise in the back of his throat.

Durant shrugged. "We're not sure, but we don't think so. All we know is that Miller escaped and fled to London. We know he spoke with the Lords Proprietors and told them Johnny had embezzled all of the king's tax money. They sent for Johnny and he went there to explain otherwise. Of course, we didn't have all the receipts we needed to prove no one embezzled, as the colony was in complete chaos for the first few months we took over, and the records from before we took over were incomplete and filled with discrepancies. Johnny sent word to us that he had met with Lord Shaftesbury and the other Lords Proprietors and that everything was in order. He was arrested shortly after he sent the letter, so the only thing we can figure is that Miller didn't get satisfaction from the Lord Proprietors with his tale of being ousted, so he went to the Privy Council with the same story, and the Privy Council took him seriously."

John's forehead furrowed. "So, the charge is from the king? A charge of embezzlement against the king is treasonous."

"The Lords Proprietors agreed that most of the money was accounted for and they would wait for the rest. They should be able to help straighten this out and get Johnny out of jail," Bird said.

Durant shook his head. "But if they were going to help, you'd think they would've already done so. Johnny's been sitting in jail for months. I don't think the Lords Proprietors have any intention of helping him."

"Then someone needs to go there and convince them otherwise," John said. "I'll sail as soon as I can find a ship. I need you to gather as much customs and tax information in writing as you have so I can take it with me."

"Everything we had is already there. Johnny took it with him," Durant said.

Bird nodded.

"Would either of you come with me to act as a witness?" John asked.

Bird and Durant glanced at each other and both shook their heads.

Durant said, "What if Johnny isn't the only person Miller wants to file charges against? We don't want to find ourselves in the same position."

John nodded. "You're probably right."

CHAPTER 28

Lord Shaftesbury

John took a seat across the massive table from his childhood friend Anthony Ashley-Cooper, the earl of Shaftesbury and the head of the Lords Proprietors of Carolina. After a servant poured them goblets of wine and left the room, Lord Shaftesbury spoke. "John, I'm sure you're here about the predicament your son is in, but I'm not sure how I can help."

"My son is being brought to trial on the charge that he seized the king's customs without authority."

Lord Shaftesbury frowned. "There's nothing I can do about that. The Lords Proprietors didn't give him authority to collect the funds, and even though he has presented most of the receipts, he still wasn't authorized to take the money. We didn't press charges against him, as we'd rather keep this matter private, but the Privy Council got word of it from Miller and they filed charges. From this side of the ocean, you have to admit it looks like Johnny conspired to defraud the king, and also he admitted that he was one of the people who incited the citizens of Albemarle to rebellion. Ultimately, it's a rebellion against the king and the proprietors. He's admitted to being one of the leaders, so how can I tell the court anything different? Am I supposed to lie to the Privy Council? I would find myself facing my own charges, and I would certainly lose my position with the Lords Proprietors."

"You're going to lose more than that if my son is convicted. The king won't look too kindly upon the blundering mess you've made of Albemarle. After the rebellion in Jamestown, I'm confident the king has grown weary of these disorderly colonies. He'll certainly take Albemarle, your proprietorship, and perhaps even your title. This whole situation is your fault for not controlling the colony the way you were supposed to, the way the king expected you to."

Lord Shaftesbury sighed. "I know you're right, my friend. But I still don't see how I can help you. If Johnny doesn't produce receipts for all of the customs he has collected, then he has indeed embezzled the king's funds."

"Would it be better for you to come up with some receipts and save your proprietorship, or would you rather remain silent and see my son's head on a spike simply to justify your blunder? If you could see the chaos that's happening in the colonies, you would understand that my son is the only reason you still have a colony at all. My boy is the key to saving your proprietorship, but not if he's hanged."

Lord Shaftesbury stroked his beard. "I'm listening," he said.

CHAPTER 29

Trial of Johnny Culpepper

The sergeant at arms escorted Johnny to a chair in the middle of the courtroom at Westminster. Two rows of men in black robes faced him from the tables at the head of the room. Guards lined the stone walls and spectators watched from the benches. All eyes were upon Johnny as he nervously took his seat.

The magistrate rose from the center of the head table and cleared his throat. "John Culpepper Junior, you have been charged with treason for embezzling the king's rightful duties and customs from the colony of Albemarle. How do you plead?"

John rose from his seat directly behind his son. "If it pleases the court, I am John Culpepper Senior and I represent the interests of John Culpepper Junior. He pleads not guilty."

"Very well, Mr. Culpepper. Let it be known that the defendant pleads not guilty." The magistrate sat down. "To open this proceeding, the gentlemen of the bench would like to hear the testimony of Mr. Thomas Miller. Mr. Miller, please come forward and state your case."

Miller rose and strutted to the center of the courtroom, his heels clicking loudly. He sneered at Johnny as he passed him. He sat in a chair to the right of the gentlemen of the court.

"Do you have testimony to offer, Mr. Miller?" the magistrate asked.

"Yes, I do."

"Please proceed," the magistrate said.

"This man," he pointed at Johnny, "kidnapped me and all the members of my cabinet and held us in prison for nearly two years, while he and his band of rebels took over the county of Albemarle in the colony of Carolina. They acted as governors and even judges, and Johnny Culpepper personally acted as the tax collector for the county. He took money from the citizens and the merchants, money that obviously belongs to the king, and used it for his own benefit."

The magistrate looked at John. "Mr. Culpepper, as council for the accused, do you have questions for Mr. Miller regarding his statement?"

"Yes, sir, I do."

"You may proceed."

John rose and walked toward Miller. "Do you have proof of your accusations, Mr. Miller?"

"Which part? That I was kidnapped, or that Johnny Culpepper has been embezzling the king's funds?"

"Let's start with the alleged kidnapping. Why were you in Albemarle?"

"I was the acting governor in the absence of Thomas Eastchurch."

"Who is Mr. Eastchurch?"

"He was the appointed governor of Albemarle by the Lords Proprietors."

"Were you granted any position by the Lords Proprietors?"

"No."

"You were escorting Mr. Eastchurch?"

"Yes."

"Can you tell the court, Mr. Miller, why you were in Albemarle without Mr. Eastchurch? Where was he?"

"He was detained in Nevis, so I went ahead to Albemarle to run the county until he arrived."

"Who gave you the commission to govern the county?"

"I wasn't exactly given the commission. Mr. Eastchurch was the acting governor, but he personally asked me to hold the position until he arrived."

"Do you have this in writing?"

"No, sir. It was a verbal agreement."

"So you entered Albemarle and took over the government without written authority?"

"It was a verbal agreement."

"Perhaps we could hear from Mr. Eastchurch. Where is he now?"

"I'm afraid he died on his way to Albemarle."

"So, the colony was without representation and leadership, without their appointed governor?"

"Well, I was there to oversee things."

"But you were not legally authorized to do so."

"Only by Mr. Eastchurch's wishes."

"But not by the Lords Proprietors."

"No."

"Very well, then, let's move on. Do you have any proof that Johnny Culpepper did not file the receipts for the customs he collected with the Lords Proprietors?"

"I know for a fact that he has not filed any customs receipts with the Lords Proprietors because they don't exist."

"You say you were held prisoner for nearly two years?"

"Yes."

"Then how would you know which receipts exist and which don't?"

Miller did not answer.

"That's all right, I don't require an answer

for that question. We will hear later directly from the Lords Proprietors about the validity of your claim. Can you tell us what happened to the taxes you collected while you were illegally acting as governor and tax collector?"

"My tenure wasn't illegal."

"Nevertheless, what happened to the tax monies you collected?"

"I was going to turn them over to the Lords Proprietors, but I was kidnapped at gunpoint and held in a filthy barn against my wishes. The money I collected ended up in the hands of Culpepper and his cohorts."

"Do you know for a fact that Mr. Culpepper didn't turn over the money to the Lords Proprietors?"

"I do not."

"One more question before you are finished. Are you the one who filed charges against this man?" He pointed to Johnny.

"I am."

"Were they charges for illegally taking over the colony, illegally collecting taxes, and not reporting said taxes?"

"Yes."

"That's very interesting, Mr. Miller." John paused for a moment as he allowed the members of the council to see the irony in Miller's charges. After a moment, he said, "It seems to me the one who was illegally taking over the colony, illegally collecting taxes, and who did not report said taxes is you, Mr. Miller. I have no more questions." He walked past Johnny and took his seat.

The magistrate's forehead wrinkled as he glared at Miller. "Do you have any proof that Mr. Culpepper has withheld funds from the Lords Proprietors or the king?"

"No, sir."

"You may take your seat, Mr. Miller," said the magistrate.

The spectators mumbled as Miller shuffled past Culpepper, his step not as grand as when he first appeared. Johnny ignored him, staring straight ahead.

"Mr. Culpepper, as attorney for the accused, would you care to call a witness in defense?"

John rose. "I would, your honor. I would like to call Lord Shaftesbury as a witness."

"Lord Shaftesbury, please step forward," the magistrate called.

The large and formidable man rose and walked to the center of the room. He quickly patted Johnny's shoulder as he passed him.

John cleared his throat. "Lord Shaftesbury, would you please tell the court your involvement in this case."

"I am the head of the Lords Proprietors of Carolina. I am the contact for taxes and customs collected in the county."

"Can you tell us about Mr. Miller's post in

the government of Albemarle?"

"I don't know what Mr. Miller is babbling on about. At no time did the Lords Proprietors ever give Mr. Miller the legal authority to rule the county. We never elected him governor, judge, or tax collector. We sent Mr. Eastchurch over as the governor, but as Mr. Miller has previously stated, Mr. Eastchurch died en route."

"Did Mr. Miller inform you of Mr. Eastchurch's death?"

"No."

"So, seeing as there was no legal entity in the county, do you consider that there was a rebellion in Albemarle?"

"From what I understand, there was a rebellion against Miller's illegal actions, but never any sort of revolt against the proprietors or the king."

"Since you did not commission Miller, did you concern yourself when the colonists turned against him?"

"No, not in the least. As a matter of fact, I would like to personally thank Mr. Culpepper for assisting us over the last few years. He and his comrades stepped in to fill the void left by Mr. Eastchurch's untimely death."

"Did Mr. Culpepper illegally collect customs in Albemarle?"

"No, Mr. Culpepper was elected tax collector by his constituents, which we understand was a fair and legal election. Since that time, he has delivered the duties and the customs receipts to us in a timely manner. The percentage of those customs due to the king will be paid promptly. There has been no impropriety in Mr. Culpepper's financial activities. These charges brought forth by Mr. Miller are preposterous, and I have letters here from the other Lords Proprietors and from a few citizens of Albemarle stating as such." Lord Shaftesbury pulled no less than a dozen pieces of paper from his breast pocket and handed them to the sergeant at arms. They were deposited on the desk in front the magistrate. "Mr. Magistrate, you have my assurance the situation in Albemarle has been settled, the king's customs will be paid forthwith, and Mr. Culpepper deserves nothing but our thanks for the way he has kept the county running smoothly in lieu of a true governor."

The magistrate shuffled through the letters, cocking his head this way and that as he read them. After a few minutes, he lifted his eyes to Johnny and nodded. "Mr. Culpepper, I'm afraid you have been summoned here for some sort of personal grudge. The charges against you will be promptly struck and you are free to go." He turned to Lord Shaftesbury. "Lord Shaftesbury, thank you for your testimony. If you have nothing else to add, you may step down." He then looked at Thomas Miller. "And, you, Mr. Miller, are only moments away from being held in contempt. It seems you have taken up the time of this court for a frivolous personal attack. I would suggest you leave this court quietly and do not show your face around here again."

Miller grimaced.

The magistrate slammed his gavel on the wooden table and rose. "This court is dismissed."

Johnny sat unmoving in his chair, his face pale. He closed his eyes and exhaled. His father approached him and pulled him to his feet. The two hugged. They were joined by Lord Shaftesbury, who shook hands with both of them.

"Lord Shaftesbury, I can't thank you enough for your help," John said.

"I'm glad you came to me first. On behalf of the Lords Proprietors, we owe you a great debt. We certainly don't want the king taking our charter, and we don't want to look incompetent in front of him. If anyone surrounding Albemarle was convicted of a treasonous activity, it would certainly reflect poorly on our ability to control the colony. I was more than happy to help you."

He turned to Johnny. "I meant every word of my testimony. I know your intentions were not as pure as I made them sound, but you and your friends have kept the county from falling into ruin during our lapse of judgment. We owe you a great debt."

"Thank you for everything, Lord Shaftesbury. I owe you a great debt in return."

"Then we're even." He patted Johnny on the shoulder and looked at John. "Will you be returning to the colonies?"

"Yes. On the next available ship!"

"Have a safe voyage, John. The other Lords Proprietors and I will see to it that Albemarle has a new and fair governor very soon. Don't kidnap this one, eh, Johnny?"

Johnny smiled. "You have my word, sir."

After Lord Shaftesbury left, John said to Johnny, "I'm heading back to Virginia. Are you going to Carolina, or would you like to come with me? You know your mother is worried sick."

"I'd like to come with you to Virginia, Father."

CHAPTER 30

Home

John stood on the bow of the ship, feeling the salt and spray blanket his face with each passing wave. His old legs wobbled with the rise and fall of the ship, making him laugh. They never did that when he sailed as a young man. So many times during his merchant days he had stood just like this on the bow and worshiped the blue horizon. So many months, even years, of his life, he had been spent away from his wife and sons. So many voyages he had longed to come home, yet when he was home he yearned to be in this very spot, feeling the warmth of the high-noon sun on his brow, watching the seagulls dance among the hemp ropes and sprawling yardarms. His face didn't have so many lines in those days, but his curls that were now gray and brittle still tangled in his collar as he held tightly on to the carved railing.

Johnny joined him. "Father, you enjoy this, don't you?"

"There is nothing I love more than the sapphire water and the endless horizon."

"When did you start sailing?"

"It was long before you were born, son. My whole life I wanted nothing more than this."

"I remember you being gone for extended periods of time when I was a child, but I don't remember ever asking Mother where you were. I guess I knew you were somewhere on the ocean."

"I'm sorry I wasn't home for you more, but I was a merchant for nearly twenty years. Merchants don't make money sitting at home."

Johnny looked out across the horizon. "I'm sorry I haven't been home more with you and Mother. I guess I just wanted to go find my own way."

"I know that, and you don't need to apologize. I was always happy to let you live your life the way you wanted. I would never stand in the way of your dreams or your contentment. My father wanted me to follow in his footsteps, to be a lawyer. He never wanted me to be a sailor. He even threatened to disown me if I became one, but I followed my own dreams anyway. I hated him for a long, long time because of that, and I never wanted you to feel the same anger."

"Your father disapproved of you sailing?

I didn't know that."

John nodded. "My father sent me to law school and I loathed every minute of it."

"But it came in handy, didn't it?"

"Yes, I guess everything in life happens for a reason." John looked across the water in silence for a few minutes. "I guess my rebellious trait was passed down to you."

"What do you mean?"

"I rebelled against my father by purchasing a ship. You were just a young boy, so I don't know if you remember, but following the war, my ship was the only thing that saved our family. We would have surely been executed if I had followed my father's dream."

"Well, that must have showed him, eh?"

John smiled a wistful grin. "I wish it were that simple." Johnny looked at him, waiting for him to continue, but he didn't have anything more to say. After a few moments of nothing more than the splash of waves across the bow, Johnny turned and walked away, leaving his father alone on the deck.

John looked up at the sky, thinking of his own father and the animosity they shared for the first twenty-seven years of John's life. There were vague remembrances of warmth and loving smiles, but they were very few. He felt his anger melting away as he realized his father was the reason Johnny was alive and free on this day, and for the first time in John's life, he felt at peace with his family and his past. "I forgive you," he whispered to the sky. A tear stung his eye as he remembered the smell of his father's shirt in a rare moment in his father's embrace. He wiped his eyes. A school of dolphins frolicked in the waves in front of the ship. "And I miss you, too."

John stood on the bow by himself for a long time, realizing his life had unfolded just as it should have. Everything has a cost. Everything has a reward. Everything happens for a reason, and even if one doesn't understand the reason at the time, one needs to know there is an ultimate purpose. Perhaps the reason will reveal itself someday, perhaps not, but every action, every emotion, every ounce of anger, of strength, of rebellion, of love will lead to the next part of the journey. John inhaled a deep breath of moist sea air and exhaled, feeling the tension drain from his shoulders. Life was good.

John looked up at a sailor in the crow's nest and imagined it to be his old first mate Benjamin. He smiled as he thought, "Take us home, Benjamin. Take us home."

THE END

Author's Notes

This book stems from decades of genealogical research by me and others. I found that in the late 1500s, there were more than a dozen Culpepper barons and earls living in England. They had enormous wealth, vast land holdings, and great manor houses, many of which are still standing today. This was the privilege John Culpepper was born into. I wondered how and why, when they possessed such great power and prestige, they chose to sail across the ocean, move to an inhospitable land, and face possible starvation and death. Why would they leave the comfort of their manors and servants to live in probable squalor and battle savage Indians? How did they end up becoming the modest people I knew in my youth in Mississippi? We discovered the answers to those questions in the second book of the Culpepper Saga, *John Culpepper the Merchant*, when a disastrous civil war in England ran the royalist family out of the country. They had no choice but to flee England, and probably with only the clothes upon their backs.

As I researched the family, I ran into the problem most Culpepper researchers run into. Each man named John had a brother named Thomas. Each John and Thomas had sons named John and Thomas. As the family grew, cousins and second cousins were all named John and Thomas, and they occasionally married within the family, creating a whole new tangled web of Culpepper history. The records blurred. The history became confusing. English records were destroyed. Colonial records were incomplete. After committing the known timelines of all the different Johns and Thomases to paper, I believe I have sorted out which one was which. In an attempt to keep them straight in the reader's mind, I have given some of them nicknames such as Johnny in this story, yet they are all listed in historical records as John or Thomas. Of course, as new documents are uncovered, it is possible that my theory is just as mistaken as theories that have come before.

John Culpepper the Merchant was the first in the family to migrate to America. This four-book series begins on the day John was born and concludes at the end of his life, but John's is not the only story here. There are far too many religious and political events and bold and brave personalities surrounding the family to ignore. These events and people shaped the man we know as John Culpepper. This series uncovers a life of passion, heroism and bravery, love and forgiveness, and ultimately truth. Truth of our history and truth about life itself.

John Culpepper is believed to be the progenitor of all American Culpeppers. He was my tenth great-grandfather.

In this story, John is a remarkable seventy-six years old. There is no record of John's death or burial as far as I know. There was a John Culpepper who died in 1674 in Virginia, but he was the sheriff of Northampton and his will states he had no children. If this was our hero, he would have been sixty-eight at the time, which I feel is quite a considerable age to be the sheriff, and we know that John had children. So, I suspect the record is referring to John's nephew, son of his brother Thomas, the character I nicknamed JJ in *John Culpepper, Esquire*. There is also no record of John's wife after the family left England in 1650. It's possible she never even made it to Virginia, either dying during the English civil war or on the voyage to Virginia. Perhaps someday, someone will find some definitive records.

The events surrounding Alex, Margaretta, and the baby Catherine are not proven, but I find it strange that Alex spent his whole life living at Leeds Castle with Margaretta, that she had a child by an absentee husband who lived openly with his mistress and had two children by her, and that Margaretta's child was named Catherine when Alex's mother Katherine died two years prior to the child's birth. I also find it interesting that Alex left everything in his will to Margaretta. Catherine later married Lord Thomas Fairfax, the fifth baron of Cameron, and Alex left his one-sixth proprietorship of Virginia to Catherine's firstborn son. The final interesting point from this tangled history is that Alex, Margaretta, and Catherine are all buried at Broomfield Church near Leeds Castle, while Margaretta's husband and Catherine's husband are buried elsewhere.

Below are some interesting facts that take place after this story ends.

Valentine Bird died at the end of the Carolina rebellion in 1679. Johnny returned to Albemarle upon being acquitted and married Valentine Bird's widow, Margaret. The Birds had a daughter named Sarah, who was a minor at the time of Valentine's death. There is some evidence that Johnny had a biological daughter named Sarah Culpepper, but I believe this girl was Valentine Bird's daughter, as it was custom at the time for minors to take the stepfather's surname. Johnny and Margaret moved to a plantation in Pasquotank Precinct, where they lived a quiet life with Johnny being a merchant/planter. Margaret died in 1687 and Johnny married a woman named Sarah Mayo in 1688. Johnny died sometime before February

1694, when records show Sarah Mayo remarried. The records state that Johnny had two or more children, listed only as "the orphans of John Culpeper."

In 1680, Frances married her third husband, Colonel Philip Ludwell of the four-thousand-acre Rich Neck Plantation. Ludwell had been a chief supporter of Berkeley during the rebellion and also Berkeley's cousin. Frances never relinquished her title, however, and was known as Lady Frances Berkeley for the remainder of her life. Philip Ludwell became the governor of Carolina in 1691. Lady Berkeley died in 1695 at the age of sixty-one. Her body is interred at Jamestown Church Cemetery in Jamestown and a portion of her headstone is still visible. She had no children.

In a side note, Thomas Miller took an appointment as customs collector in England in March of 1681 and was soon arrested and imprisoned for embezzlement. He died in prison in 1685.

My deepest thanks go out to those who made this book possible:

Elyse Dinh-McCrillis—TheEditNinja.com

Robert Hess—book designer

Warren Culpepper and Lew Griffin, who maintain the Culpepper Connections website, and all of the Culpepper descendants who contribute to it.

Books by Lori Crane

Okatibbee Creek Series
Okatibbee Creek
An Orphan's Heart
Elly Hays

Stuckey's Bridge Trilogy
The Legend of Stuckey's Bridge
Stuckey's Legacy: The Legend Continues
Stuckey's Gold: The Curse of Lake Juzan

Culpepper Saga
I, John Culpepper
John Culpepper the Merchant
John Culpepper, Esquire
Culpepper's Rebellion

Other Titles
Savannah's Bluebird
The Culpepper-Fairfax Scandal
Witch Dance
On This Day: A Perpetual Calendar for Family Genealogy

About the Author

Bestselling and award-winning author Lori Crane is a writer of southern historical fiction and the occasional thriller. Her books have climbed to the Kindle Top 100 lists many times, with *Elly Hays* debuting on Amazon at #1 in Native American stories. She has also enjoyed a place among her peers in the Top 100 historical fiction authors on Amazon, climbing to #23. She is a native Mississippi belle currently residing in greater Nashville.

She is a member of the Daughters of the American Revolution, the United States Daughters of 1812, the United Daughters of the Confederacy, and the Historical Novel Society. She is also a professional musician and member of the Screen Actors Guild-American Federation of Television and Radio Artists.

Visit Lori's website at
www.LoriCrane.com

Sign up for Lori's quarterly newsletter at
http://eepurl.com/GHJ7D

Excerpt from

Okatibbee Creek

the first in the Okatibbee Creek Series

September 1834, Mississippi

"Help! Help! Somebody! James! Susannah!"

We all run as fast as we can down the creek toward the screaming, hopping over rocks and stumps and each other. When we arrive at the clearing, we see him next to the creek, dripping wet, on his hands and knees over the lifeless body of William. About twenty feet away lies Stephen, his clothes soaking wet, his head cocked to one side, and his left arm bent uncomfortably under his back. His lifeless eyes are staring into the darkening treetops.

Susannah starts screaming, but everyone ignores her. James runs directly to Stephen, picks him up by his shoulders, and starts shaking him, but it is painfully obvious that our Stephen is gone. His lips are blue. He isn't moving. He isn't breathing.

James yells at Susannah to stop screaming, and to run to the house and get Daddy. Susannah doesn't move, but her screaming quiets to a whimper.

James stands up and yells at her again. "Go, Susannah, go! Go get Daddy!"

I feel ice in my veins at the tone of James's voice. Susannah still doesn't move.

One of my brothers runs over to James's side and starts to pick up Stephen under his arms. "Help me pick him up, James. We don't have time for Susannah to go all the way there and back! Let's just get them back to the house," he urges.

They lift Stephen and carry his body toward the darkening woods, in the direction that leads back to the house. My other brothers follow their lead, pick William up under his arms and legs, and quickly move in the same direction.

Susannah stands frozen like a statue in the same spot, whimpering with her hands over her mouth. I run up behind her and nudge her toward the woods.

"Let's go, Sue. We have to run."

She doesn't move. She's white as a sheet. I push harder with my trembling hands.

"Sue! Now! Let's go!"